J. S. Dye

**Humanity**

Its fountain and stream

J. S. Dye

**Humanity**
*Its fountain and stream*

ISBN/EAN: 9783337370848

Printed in Europe, USA, Canada, Australia, Japan

Cover: Foto ©Andreas Hilbeck / pixelio.de

More available books at **www.hansebooks.com**

# FOUNTAIN AN͏̲D ͏STREAM.

## BY
## DEACON

*ILLUSTRATED BY ONE HU̲̅RAVINGS,*

GIVING ONE TRUE AND COR

### TAKEN FROM

OF EACH DISTINCT PEOPLE NOW KNOW̲̅IZED WORLD:

AMONG WHICH

*THE REIGNING SOVEREIGNS PRESIDENT*
*GRANT, AND OT̲*

EACH PORTRAIT, AT GREAT EXPENSE, IS CAR̲̅LORED WITH A
BRUSH, BY HAND, GIVING THE EXA̲̅STINCT
PEOPLE IN THEIR

NEW YORK:
**PUBLISHED BY THE AUTHOR,**
648 BROADWAY.
1870.

Entered according to Act of Congress, in the year 1870, in the Clerk's Office of the District Court of the United States for the Southern District of New York.

LITTLE, RENNIE & Co., Stereotypers, 645 and 647 Broadway, New York.

# PREFACE.

We give in the following pages the results of a quarter of a century's research and investigation, condensed, it is true, but yet exhibiting such a comprehensive view of the subject as we trust cannot fail of being interesting, instructive, and popular. Not being content with gambolling along the banks of the expanded stream, we have everywhere endeavored to explore up to the fountain head. From the facts we have gathered, our conclusions differ in many respects from those of others who have examined and written on the same subject.

But, nevertheless, we fearlessly submit them with candor and confidence to the judgment of the present enlightened and inquiring age ; not forgetting in the mean time that others, high in the confidence of their fellowmen, have arrived at different conclusions, and entertain different views.

The facts and arguments used to demonstrate the true cause of difference between the apparent distinct families of mankind being founded on facts, must, we think, stand the test of the most rigid investigation. If we have discovered the key that opens the casket containing the secret of the different complexions among men, then the Portraits, produced at great expense in the body of the work, when stripped of their different complexions, must ever remain an unanswerable argument in favor of the brotherhood of man.

We might have produced portraits of men of the lowest grade of the different types of the human family, and contrasted them with the highest order of the same type ; and the difference would be actually as great, if not greater, than between a highly cultivated African (leaving out the complexion and hair) and an Englishman.

Reader, whatever may be the color of your skin, look back with us through the dim ages of the past, and we will show you that the Human Family had a *common origin*, spoke but *one language*, and once occupied *within the Tropics a common home*, and had at that time but *one complexion.*

We have also, by arduous research, become thoroughly convinced that the pagan world, long before the Jews were a distinct people, had traditions of the creation, the flood, and a hope of life beyond the grave. To establish these truths, we have given lengthy quotations from many of the ancient pagan authors, some of them living before the time of Moses. We have gathered facts wherever we could find them, and the reader may rely on it, that every extract quoted is from the best and most reliable ancient authorities.

We hope by our humble efforts to have been the instrument of bringing to light some heretofore undiscovered facts concerning the early history of man ; facts that may in some future age be enlarged, so as to open up to the human understanding all that in this life can be learned concerning the early history of Adam and his posterity.

DEACON DYE.

# CONTENTS OF PART FIRST.

# HUMANITY:

## ITS FOUNTAIN AND STREAM.

HAVING long been a student, MAN has at last become
a study. Hope, his natural inheritance, imparted to him
at birth by his suffering, yet hopeful mother, remains his
life-long companion. But knowledge he can only acquire
by patient study and ardent investigation. Let us first,
then, endeavor to trace the connection between all created
beings, and discover, if possible, the *plan* of the Creator
in relation to Man. It is the noblest work of science,
through the study of natural laws, to lead the doubtful
skeptic up to see and appreciate his God. The study
of the animal kingdom, during the last century, became
almost perfect by the great French naturalist Cuvier's
discovery, that it was constructed upon a *plan*. He
showed that all animals, however diversified, are built on
four plans. And all investigation since his day has confirmed the truth of his discovery. These four great divi-
sions are known under the names of *Radiates*, *Mollusks*,
*Articulates*, and *Vertebrates*. The German transmutation doctrine assumes that animals are derived from one
another ;—all Radiates from one primitive *Radiate ;* all
Mollusks from one primitive *Mollusk ;* all Articulates
from one primitive *Articulate ;* and all Vertebrates from
one primitive *Vertebrate :* and these primitive types are

all derived from a primitive *cell*, which was formed by the conditions of the elements bringing into life organized beings wherever light, moisture, and matter are brought into contact. *Moleschatt, Vogt, Buchner,* and *Czolbe,* contended for this theory. The paper of the first, on the action of light upon matter in organizing beings, stands pre-eminent in *that school.*

Darwin and the English defenders of the transmutation doctrine, present it in somewhat different light. They assume that the first impulse was given by an *Intelligent Power,* and from this impulse has resulted, not only the first germs of creation, but all that have followed. Now the subject to be considered is, whether the unintelligent transmutation doctrine of the German philosophers, or the intellectual transmutation theory of Darwin, or the Bible doctrine of special creation, is correct. If this last is correct, then is established the fact, that we are not the lineal descendants of monkeys, but the chosen production of a powerful *mind*—the children of God, made in his resemblance.

We might go into an examination of the remains of animals found in the various geological strata of the earth. How that we have some of the lowest forms rising higher at the same time, so that we should have, according to the transmutation doctrine, beings capable of changing themselves, and at the same time remaining as they were; at the same time influences which would produce the change, and also prevent the change from going on. This is not logical, and a doctrine that has facts against it so glaring is not a correct interpretation of Nature. Man did not spring up from the earth, because the earth had become what it was. But the earth was prepared for man that he might grow and find an appropriate home for his increase and development.

Ever since the time of Aristotle, animals having a backbone, such as quadrupeds, birds, reptiles, and fishes, have been called Vertebrates. It required close investigation, and great knowledge of anatomy, to discover that the snake which crawls, the bird which flies, the dog which runs, and the fish which swims, were all built on the same plan. In viewing the external development of the vertebrates, or backboned tribe, we are struck with their differences, yet their internal structures are arranged the same, and the different parts are combined together in the same way. The covering is different;—the fish may have scales, the bird feathers, and the quadruped hair. But if you examine the early growth of the feathers in the young bird, or scales on the young fish, or hair on the young quadruped, you will see scarcely any difference. The arm of a man and the limb of any quadruped are formed on the same plan. Thus, man's arm consists, first, of a triangular bone, called the shoulder-blade, from which projects another bone called the collar-bone; then we have the upper-arm bone, which extends to the elbow; then two parallel bones extending from the elbow to the wrist; then five, which form the palm; then the thumb with two joints; and the fingers with three joints each. Of course, the external of these limbs show the extremes. All animals have not five fingers; some have but four, some three, others only two. The horse walks on tiptoe, on one finger. Among reptiles, instead of three joints of the finger, there are a larger number; and instead of five, there are six fingers. Occasionally a human being has been born with six fingers and six toes. Among animals

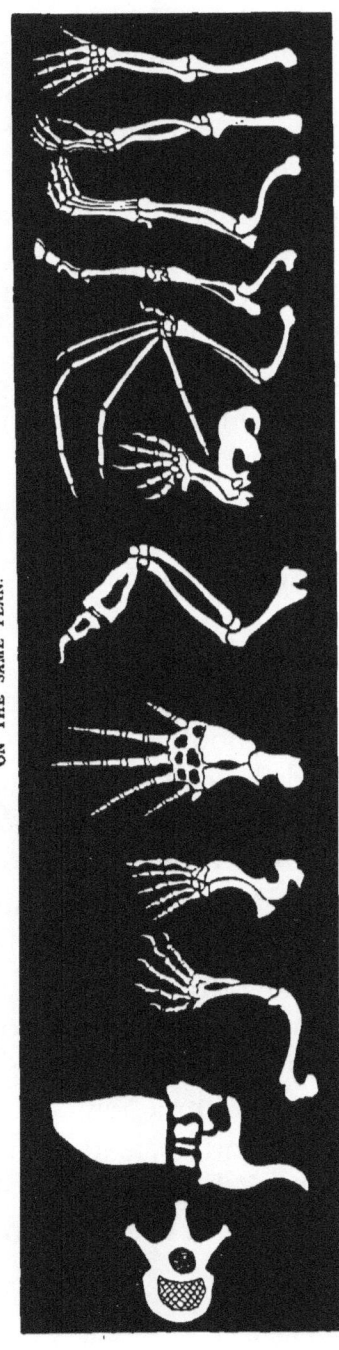

ALL THE VERTIBRATE TRIBES, AS SHOWN BY THIS ENGRAVING, WERE CONSTRUCTED BY PROVIDENCE ON THE SAME PLAN.

ARM OF A MAN.

Completion of the original design.

ARM OF A GORILLA.

LEG OF A DOG.

LEG OF A SHEEP.

WING OF A BAT.

LEG OF A MOLE.

WING OF A BIRD.

PADDLE OF A WHALE.

PADDLE OF A SEAL.

LEG OF A TURTLE.

FIN OF A FISH.

VERTIBRATE, OR PART OF A BACKBONE.

this is frequent.   In fish they go on increasing from six to twenty.   So all these small bones are only so many fingers each, divided into a great number of joints.   But after all, it is only the spreading hand in which all the joints are united in a web.   If we advance a step beyond, we find the four bones corresponding to the wrist ; then two broad bones which correspond to the fore-arm ; then a very short upper-arm bone ; then, close to the shoulder, a collar-bone and shoulder-blade, exactly as in man.   So the correspondence is complete.   (See Plate, p. 10.)   The vertebrate tribes number in all about twenty-one thousand : fish, ten thousand ; reptiles, two thousand ; birds, seven thousand ; mammals, two thousand.

Articulates embrace all the host of insects : Butterflies, Beetles, Bugs, Flies, and all the great variety of winged animals with six legs.   This division also includes Crabs, Lobsters, everything having a large number of locomotive appendages, even down to worms.   They all have rings on the surface of the body, moveable one upon the other, and jointed legs projecting from the sides of these rings ; and thus their relation is made plain by a few general features.   These number about three hundred thousand.

Then we have Mollusks, which include those soft-bodied animals, like Oysters, Clams, Snails, and Slugs. The bodies of all these are capable of great expansion and contraction, and are generally covered with a shelly envelope.   Numbering about twenty thousand.

Last, the Radiates, numbering about ten thousand. This plan embraces the Star-fishes, Sea-urchins, Jelly-fishes, Corals, and animals of that character.   They are built on a plan totally different and distinct to the other three, and show a powerful and comprehensive mind expressing through a multitude of forms, and varying the forms in a multitude of ways, so as to express the same thought. When we consider the whole animal kingdom, consisting of hundreds of thousands of different kinds of beings constituted only on four plans, and how these plans must necessarily be expressed in thousands of different ways, we are not surprised at the labor it cost man to discover them. But there is no living creature on the face of the earth, but can easily be traced to one of these four plans. I think facts will warrant the assertion, that each of these plans shows development as well as variation. The Vertebrates plan, all naturalists agree, commences with Fishes, of which species the Lamper Eel is the lowest type, and the Shark and Skate the highest.

We now come to examine the Reptiles. We place the Salamander the lowest, and Tortoises the highest. Then come the Birds, the lowest of which are those hardly able to fly, such as the Penguin, and the Eagle the highest.

First, then, we have Fishes ; second, Reptiles ; third, Birds ; and last, Mammals. The lowest of this class are the Whales ; they are not properly fish,—having lungs, a double circulation, and warm blood ; it brings forth living young, and nurses them with milk, like quadrupeds ; they belong to the same class of animals to which man belongs, only they are the lowest.

We have made these extended remarks on the animal kingdom in order to explain how the Almighty had a plan, and that Man was not an after consideration, but occupied the highest position in His purposes and plans. To prove this fact we must consult the science of Geology.

These beautiful lines, composed on the early formation of animal life on our globe, are descriptive and instructive.

### HYMN OF THE CORALS.

"Beneath the realm which the waves o'erwhelm,
In the seas of the torrid zone,
Our ancient race have a dwelling-place,
In a world that is all our own.

Earth boasts no spots like the fairy grots
Where we build our sparry cell;
Nor can its bowers produce such flowers
As in depths of ocean dwell.

And our forms so strange we ever change,
As over the deep we roam;
And our varied hue is ever new,
As we vary our ocean home.

In tranquil calms, we wave like palms,
Or bend like the drooping willow:
Or we climb to the verge of the foaming surge,
And dash to the winds its billow.

In peaceful haunts, like tender plants,
We twine our fragile forms;
Or we build a rock to the tempest's shock,
That mocks its fiercest storms.

And we rear the walls of those marble halls
As a precipice high and steep,

Till a new-found isle is seen to smile
Like a beacon o'er the deep.

By viewless hands those new-born lands
Are strewn with blessings rife;
Till man appears, and claims the spheres
To being raised and life.

And we join the piles of those fossil isles
Till they spread from shore to shore;
And we build from the caves of the ocean waves
A world unknown before.

Then say, proud man, how poor the plan
Of thy pyramids, castles, and towers;
How vain the boasts of thy mightiest hosts,
Or their labors,--compared with ours!

Though such our lot, yet we are—what,
In the scale of being vast?—
The meanest germs of life's poor worms,—
The lowest and the last!

Yet, though obscure, and low, and poor,
And lost in distance dim,
We still can raise our Maker's praise,
And pour our thanks to him."

Now, the lowest of those geological systems or beds that contain no animal remains, is called *Azoic*. Upon them are deposited the first formation that contains animal remains, which is known in the system as Taconic, then Carntrain, then Silurian; then comes Devonian; then the Carboniferous, the Permian, the Triassic, the Jurassic, the Cretaceous, the Eocene, Miocene, and Pliocene; and last, the present Alluvium, in which deposits are still going on. Now, these different sets of beds all mark epochs (with their peculiar animal and vegetable remains) in the history of our globe. The igneous and primary rocks in our country constitute mainly the hills of New England; and the mountain group, in the northern part of New York, also the Blue Ridge and its collateral elevations, extending southwest through the Atlantic States. The transition and secondary rocks, especially the former, constitute the greater portion of the interior of the United States west of New England. The tertiary deposits constitute a large portion of the shores and low country of the States south of New England and bordering on the Gulf of Mexico. The alluvial deposits are found in the Western States. On the lowest layer on which animal remains have been found we discover Radiates, Mollusks, and Articulates. Although no Mammals, Birds, or Reptiles are found, yet Fishes, the last type of the Vertebrates, are represented, showing the early purposes of the Creator in relation to man, whose final appearance on the globe, as the last created being, was the crowning glory of creation.

The plan of man's organization we find began with the fish. The brain in the fish is only a slight swelling, scarcely raised above the spinal marrow, which extends through the whole backbone, and the posterior division of the brain is the highest. In the reptile the brain is slightly raised above the level of the spine, which permits the Tortoise, Lizard, and Snake to raise their heads. In birds, the anterior portion of the brain is the largest, and the posterior the smallest, with slanting position of the spine. In quadrupeds we have still further progress, until we come to man. Here we find the brain so organized that the anterior portion covers and protects all the rest so completely that nothing is seen outside; and the brain stands vertically poised on the backbone.

| | | RADIATES. | MOLLUSKS. | ARTICULATES. | VERTEBRATES. |
|---|---|---|---|---|---|
| **TERTIARY FORMATIONS.** | PRESENT. | Vegetable Soil. Beds of Gravel and Sand. Diluvium with Boulders. | | | MAN |
| | PLIOCENE. | Millstone. Sandstones. | | | |
| | MIOCENE. | Gypsum. Coarse Limestone. | | | |
| | EOCENE. | Plastic Clay. | | | MAMMALS |
| **SECONDARY FORMATIONS.** | CRETACEOUS. | Chalk Beds. Oolitic Group and Lias. | | | |
| | Jurassic. | Shell Limestone | | | MARSUPIALS |
| | TRIASSIC. | Magnesian Limestone. | | | BIRDS |
| | PERMIAN. | New Red Sandstone. | | | |
| | CARBONIFEROUS. | Coal Beds. | | INSECTS | REPTILES |
| **PRIMARY FORMATIONS.** | DEVONIAN. | Coal mixed with Sandstone. | | | |
| | SILURIAN. | Mountain Limestone. Old Red Sandstone. | | | |
| | CAMBRIAN. | Grauwacke Sandy Slate. | | | |
| | TACONIC. | Inferior stratified Rocks, Mica Slate, Gneiss, Unstratified Rocks, Granite. | | | FISH |
| | | Polyps. Acalephs. Echinoderms. | Acephala, Cephalopoda, Gasteropoda. Worms. Crustacea. | | |

Beyond this there is no further progress, showing that
man has reached the highest development of the plan
upon which his structure was laid.   We can trace progress in another aspect.   The fish swims horizontally ; his
head does not rise above the rest of his body, and there
is no contraction behind to make the neck.   The reptile
has a slight contraction behind the head, and you can tell
where the body ends and the neck begins ; yet he has no
limbs to raise his body, and uses his backbone as a pro-
pelling power.   The Lizard, where rudimentary legs
appear, is sometimes capable of raising the body slightly.
Then we come to the bird, whose tendency is to an
upright position.   The bird stands on its hind limbs ;
yet it has not entirely reached that position ; and it
requires one step more by which *one pair of limbs alone*
*are made to perform the function of locomotion, while*
*the other pair become subservient to the mind.*   Thus
the hand of man is no longer a paw, or organ of locomotion, but with it he expresses his deepest feelings, by
grasping his fellow-being in cordial recognition : while his
brain is not only forward in the way of progress in intellectual culture, but upward in the direction of all moral
excellence, he can raise his brow to heaven and contem-
plate his Maker.   His brain compares with those of the
lesser creations ; and it was demonstrated that although the
whale's and the elephant's were seemingly larger, and with
extraneous matter were heavier, yet, when the real brain
of the elephant, for example, was compared with that of
a full-grown man, it was not really so heavy, in the proportion of size of body.   His heart beats on an average
sixty to seventy times a minute.   Every beat sends forward two ounces of the fluid.   It rushes at the rate of

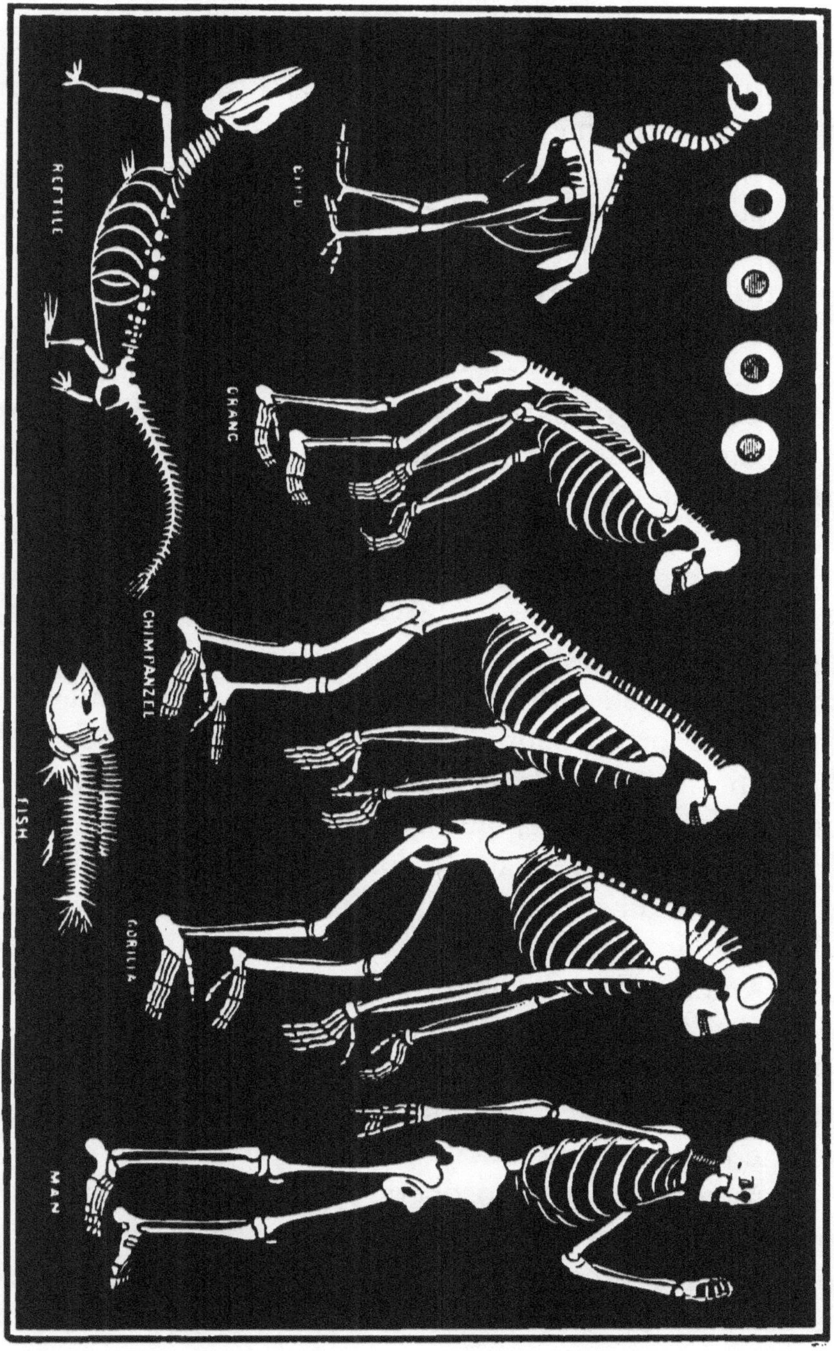

THE PLAN OF PROVIDENCE IN CONSTRUCTING THE ANIMAL KINGDOM.—MAN THE ONLY EARTHLY BEING THAT STANDS ERECT ON TWO FEET.

one hundred and fifty feet in a minute, and the whole blood passes through the lungs every two minutes and a half, or twenty times in an hour.

Thus Man stands at the head of the mundane creation, differing from all other creatures, and master of all. The entire animal and vegetable kingdoms have their geographical homes or limits, to go beyond which is death. But how different is Man! He is a cosmopolite, and can live amidst polar snows, with nine months darkness, or at the Equator beneath scorching suns, or equal days and nights. Dutchmen and Russians have lived for years at seventy-eight degrees north latitude. And English and American explorers, Franklin, Kane, and Hall, have approached the eightieth degree, and the cold so intense as to freeze whiskey as hard as granite ; the thermometer standing at seventy-eight below zero. At the commencement of October, the Musk Ox and Reindeer leave for the south ; and as the sun sinks below the horizon, the great Polar Bear, who appears to have been created for this clime, lifts aloft his arctic head, snuffs the bitter cold, and retreats to his snowy den. Amid this dreadful weather the Esquimaux Indian can go to the chase. Man can endure a corresponding degree of heat. All America is inhabited to Tierra del Fuego. On the deserts of Orinoco, in the Republic of Venezuela, South America, the thermometer stands all day at one hundred and twenty degrees, yet that region contains a population of one hundred and ninety thousand souls.

In sustaining atmospheric pressure, man has great power. At twelve thousand feet above the level of the sea, the pressure on the outer surface of the body is shown by the barometer to be twenty-one thousand

## China.

LAOU, Gov. General of Canton, 1852.—This is an excellent picture of the ruling class of China. Crozier, the historian, dates the commencement of the Chinese empire 2958 years B. C. It is now divided into 18 provinces, a maritime and 15 inland, covering an area of 5,300,000 square miles, and having a population of about 400,000,000. Form of government, despotic, under an Emperor. It is administered by Mandarins, all of whom he selects from the literary class. RELIGION: The literary men are generally philosophical Atheists, the uneducated follow Buddhism. Printing, Gunpowder, and the Mariner's Compass were first known to the Chinese. The great wall, built to prevent the frontier from invasion by the Tartars, 217 years B. C., is 1,500 miles long, 20 feet in height, 25 feet thick at the bottom and 15 across the top. It is fortified, and garrisoned by a gate and tower every 300 feet. It yet remains as one of the most stupendous monuments of human industry extant.

## Asia.

NATIVE OF TIBET.—The home of the above race is on the loftiest plateau of the globe, situated between Independent Tartary on the west, Mongolia on the north, Chinese Tartary on the east, and Hindostan and Burmah on the south, between the 30th and 50th degrees latitude North, and 90th and 110th longitude east (from Ferro). Here all the animals are found wild which man has tamed: the cow, horse, ass, sheep, goat, pig, dog, cat, and even the reindeer. Adelung, Lawrence, and Blumenbach, contend that the garden of Eden was located here.

## Java.

A NATIVE OF JAVA of high rank. Taken from Raffles' History of Java: London edition. One of the Malaysian or East India islands. The natives are under a Suzerain or Emperor, and a Sultan. The Dutch occupy the portion of the North coast. The South coast is valuable from its edible birds-nests. They are mostly found in the limestone caverns, and are composed of a glutinous substance supposed to be masticated food. Large amounts of this peculiar substance are exported to China, where it is considered a choice article of food by the Mandarins. The Upas tree, of fabalistic notoriety, also grows luxuriantly here. Its juice is deadly poison to animal life. The tree grows from 60 to 200 feet high, with a white stem. The standard of beauty is very yellow complexion, with black teeth. Religion, Mohammedanism.

## Marianne Islands, East India.

MALE NATIVE.—These islands, which were discovered by Magellan in 1521, when he gave them the name of Ladrones, signifying thieves, from the thievish propensities of the people, were afterward called Marianne Islands, after Mary Ann of Austria, wife of Philip IV. of Spain, who directed their titment There are about 20 in the group, being of volcanic origin and very fertile. They are under Spanish rule, and included in the government of the Philippine Islands.

## Berber.

A NATIVE OF BARBARY.—This country lies to the west of Egypt. It is composed of Morocco, Algiers, Tunis, and Tripoli, and has the general name of Barbary, which was derived from Berbers, who held possession of it previous to the Arab conquest. The population of the country is composed of Jews, Arabs, and the old Berber stock. The portrait given is a native of Algeria, of the old Berber stock.

## Mindoro, East India.

MALE NATIVE OF THIS ISLAND.—This is one of the Philippine group, and lies south of Manilla, and near Luzon Island, in the China sea. It is thinly inhabited and under Spanish rule.

seven hundred and fifty pounds. Let him descend to the level of the sea and it is increased to thirty-two thousand three hundred and twenty-five pounds. Humboldt, in 1820, when ascending Chimborazo, found Indians living in wigwams thirteen thousand four hundred and thirty-five feet above the level of the sea. He and his Indian guide ascended nineteen thousand feet. Even this great altitude has been eclipsed by a French aeronaut who ascended twenty-two thousand nine hundred feet, which proves that man can exist one thousand nine hundred feet above the highest flight of birds. The highest flight of the Condor on the Andes being only twenty-one thousand feet.

All these different degrees may not be equally suitable and congenial to man, yet he can endure them, while the entire tribe of monkeys, including the Chimpanzee and Ourang-outang, are included in the tropics, and can only propagate in warm climates. A few of the hardier races (such as the Horse, the Ox, the Hog, the common Poultry, the Crow, the house Sparrow, and the Snipe) have a wider range as appendages to civilization ; but most of them would soon die out without its fostering care. Born into the world naked, man is the only animal that can clothe itself ; and this superior quality renders him master of all seasons and climates. From the Equator to the Poles he has the proud distinction of claiming the world as his country.

Walking erect, he uses tools, and stores knowledge, which none of the lower animals ever do. For his own use man even enslaves all of them which have a capacity for servitude, and is capable of destroying the most ferocious and dangerous among them. No savages have ever been found so destitute of ingenuity as not to be able to destroy the Elephant, the Lion, the Tiger, and Grizzly Bear.

Man is the only earthly Being that recognizes a Creator, and whether refined by civilization, or degraded by savage life, he everywhere erects altars, at which, in some form or other, he recognizes and worships the supposed author of his existence.

We have shown that Providence adopted the plan on which Man was constructed, untold ages before any geological evidence of his existence appears on the earth.

The next great question in the progress of our subject, is : " Are the different colored Races of the world, White, Red, and Black, offsprings of one original pair? or did each color have a separate and distinct origin? Agassiz divides the earth into eight geological realms, and insists that each of these realms produced its own original flora and fauna, including man, who he claims was originally created in each realm, not in pairs but in multitudes.

In looking abroad over the earth we see the human family divided into different nationalities, speaking different languages, and embracing different forms of religion. To the unreflecting mind all these peculiarities are evidences of different origin.  It readily concludes that the Circassian, Mongolian, Malay, and Negro cannot all be the posterity of Adam.  But in scientific investigation we must not jump at conclusions ; and since we have discovered in the skeleton of a fish the original prototype of man, may we not, by a little patient investigation in examining the laws of nature, arrive at correct conclusions about the plan which was adopted in intruducing man

## East Africa.

MAN OF ABYSSINIA.—Perhaps this likeness resembles the ancient Egyptian race more than any people now living. For Ethiopian descendants in Abyssinia see plate XI., No. 3.

## Fejee Islands.
A FEJEE GIRL.

## Arabia.

MOHAMMED II.—Born 1430; commenced his reign 1451, after a successful military life, wherein he conquered nearly all the nations of the East, and acquired Constantinople. Died 1481.

## India.
(BEYOND THE GANGES.)

INDO CHINAMAN, of the Southeastern peninsular of Asia: country known as Indo China Peninsular, except what belong to Great Britain. All the states in this peninsular are tributary to the Chinese empire.

## Eastern Archipelago.

MALAY MAN, a native of Borneo, one of the Sunda Islands, next to Australia.—This is the largest island in the world. The Malaysian group extends longitude 40 degrees, close to the Equator, and latitude 50 degrees, or 2,700 miles from East to West, and 2,100 miles from North to South. This picturesque blending of land and water covers an area of 5,500,000 square miles. The exact number of the islands is yet unknown. They are called by the natives *Gardens of the Sun.* The Orang Outang, a specie of man-like ape, is a native of Borneo and Sumatra, and is confined to certain localities on each, while the Chimpanzee, the other specie of man-like ape, has a wider range, and is found in Western Africa all the way from Sierra Leone to Congo. Population of Malaysia, 16,000,000 ; of Borneo, 3,000,000. The Malay is more extensively distributed over the globe than any other distinct type of man.

## Papua.

MAN NATIVE OF NEW GUINEA.—This island is 1500 miles long, and will average 300 miles in width. It lies immediately south of the Equator, and north of Australia. The natives are generally termed Oceanic Negroes, and their hair grows in separate tufts on the head. Tanaa Papua is the Malay name, meaning *Land of the crisped-haired.* It is here the gorgeous birds of Paradise have their breeding-grounds, which they periodically leave for the Spice and Nutmeg islands in the flowering season, where they get so overpowered, actually intoxicated by the odor, that they are easily captured.

into the world, which for millions of years had been pre-paring for his reception.

The color of the race, as the first pair came from the hands of the Creator, was neither *White* nor *Black*. Neither the Circassian or Negro can boast of wearing the original color of primeval man. The Bible, Science, Reason, all History and Tradition, go to prove this position true.

The best Hebrew scholars in the highest modern schools on the continent of Europe, all agree that the word Adam, when analyzed, shows two separate words, A and DAM, or A-DAM. Now A, *aleph*, is the primeval Semitic masculine article *the*, an article that in Scripture is prefixed to above forty masculine substantives; although, until recently, the fact was unperceived by Hebrew grammarians or Jewish Lexicographers. In the next place, the word *Dam* is Arabic, meaning blood, the color of which is red; consequently A, the letter *aleph*, being the masculine article *the*, and the noun *Dam* (blood), which duplex substantive, applied to man, naturally signifies the *Red Man*. And this the writer of Genesis (by applying the name Adam) asserts was the color of the first human being. Webster's definition of Adamic earth is Red Clay, " because," says he, " Adam means Red Earth." Add to this the great statistical fact that nearly two-thirds of the present inhabitants of the globe are of similar complexion, showing it is the most extensive and therefore the most natural color of the human race.

Having established that red was the primeval, and even at this day the most prevalent color of the human family, let us now try to discover, if possible, the various causes

which combined in nature to produce the *White* and
*Black* Races. We believe we have struck the key-note
which satisfactorily accounts for the different complexions.
The transit of the aboriginal color of man to the black
type, is not so great as it would be from white to black.
Neither is the transit from red to white so great as from
black to white. Through different degrees of climate,
the Almighty created a series of external causes which
existed long anterior to man, and were formed by Him
with a perfect foreknowledge of their power to change
man's complexion. If we admit God created causes
which in their own good time produce varieties, it would
be impious to suppose him so silly as to anticipate the
action of fixed laws by a new creation of white and black
races : thus superseding his original designs. Man presents no greater varieties than do animals which are
known to be of one origin. The horses, says M. Roulin,
transported to South America, have formed a race with
fur instead of hair ; and have changed to a uniform bay
color. Of two colts, says Carpenter, of the same race,
born in Lorraine and transported, one to Flanders, and
the other to Normandy, after three years the one will be a
light elegant carriage horse, while the other will be fit
only for the heaviest work, and almost incapable of a trot.
And among birds, St. Hilaire remarks, the Bullfinch
changes to black when fed on exciting food, such as
hemp-seed. The mewing of the cat and barking of the
dog are acquired by domestication ; and both become
lost in their wild state. While dogs in North India
acquire wool instead of hair ; and in Africa they become
hairless.

In 1770 and 1799, Fossil remains of the *Rhinoceros*

## Japan.

JAPANESE GIRL, Native of Yeddo.—The Japanese belong to the great Mogul Tartar family. They have broad skulls, high cheekbones, and small, black eyes. They are divided into eight classes, viz., princes, nobles, priests, soldiers, civil officers, merchants, artisans, and laborers. These are kept strict, each person always following the business or profession of his father. The women wear their hair very long, and destroy their complexion with paint; their lips they color blue, and when married they pull out their eyebrows and blacken their teeth. In 1853 Commodore Perry entered the harbor of Yeddo, and in 1854 he concluded a treaty. Yeddo, the principal city, contains a population of 2,000,000. Total population about 50,000,000. The government is military and ecclesiastical, both offices hereditary; the first, Kubo, residing at Yeddo; the second, Mikado, residing at Miako.

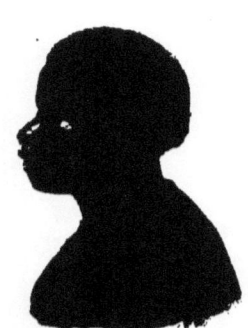

## Van Diemen's Land.

A TASMANIA WOMAN.—This is a native of the island long used by the British government as a place to transport its convicts. It lies 100 miles Southeast of Australia. The Aboriginal population is nearly all extinct. This portrait was procured years ago, and is a correct likeness of what they were.

## Hindostan.

HINDOO MAN.—The term Hindoo means "Black," therefore Hindostan signifies the country of the Blacks. But some of the Aboriginal Indian people are copper-colored, some actually pale, and others entirely black. Population about 180,000,000, of which 150,000,000 are under British rule. This portrait is that of a man of rank.

## Australia.

A MAN NATIVE OF THIS COUNTRY.—The most peculiar island or continent, in its geological, animal, and vegetable kingdoms, known on the globe. In this country everything seems totally reversed. For further description we refer the reader to Mr. Bryant's letter on the last pages of this book, under the title of NEW HOLLAND.

## Greece.

Man of the ancient Grecian type, exhibiting in his very look and form the essence of their ancient symmetry and refinement.

## New Zealand.

NEW ZEALAND CHIEF.—A group of islands in the South Pacific Ocean, belonging to Great Britain. When Capt. Cook visited their shores, he found no trace of quadrupeds, except a kind of dog, fox, and a few rats. The natives are supposed to have formerly been a branch of the Malays, and are tall, strong, and handsomely formed. The Christian missionaries have been very successful in these islands. The Aborigines have nearly all abandoned their ancient customs of cannibalism and infanticide, and embraced Christianity. They practice tattooing, and form pictures over their bodies of remarkable elegance. Total population about 160,000.

and the *Elephant* were found in Siberia encased in huge masses of ice ; one elephant had tusks ten feet long, and differed only from the *Asiatic* and *African* species by being entirely covered with hair ; and the rhinoceros was also covered with thick coarse hair, showing the mighty influence of climate in changing the external appearance of both.

The color in dark races of men originates and is contained in pigment-cells* (not membranes), and the discolorations in the white, such as the *areola mammarum* of woman, the summer freckles and moles, and brown spots which occasionally appear on the skin, all depend on the presence of cells filled with pigment, similar to those which produce the color of the Negro. These pigment-cells appear to withdraw from the blood, and elaborate in their own cavities, coloring matter of various shades, increasing and diminishing so as to form all the different hues found among the human family. By examining the skin of the Negro anatomically, says Dr. Bachman, we find no structure peculiar to it, for the very same cells are found in the fairest of mankind. And each person present knows there is such a constant relation between climate and the color of the skin, that it is impossible not to perceive the connection between them. That part of the globe included between the tropics, or closely bordering thereto, forms the exclusive seat of native black races. While the colder climates are the residence of the fairer races, and the intermediate countries are inhabited by people of Reddish, or intermediate complexion. The tribes who in the infancy of the human race migrated from temperate into hot climates, it is easily understood

* See form of cells, top of Plate, on page 17.

how, through the influence of the sun's rays and heated atmosphere, the pigment-cells that contained only a small amount of coloring matter by gradual filtration through the action of the liver began to fill up, and after countless ages of exposure to the tropical sun, the Red man, without changing his physical organization, turns gradually Black, and finally has the power to transmit that complexion to his posterity.

In other tribes who, a long time before, had migrated into northern regions where the operation of nature's laws were altogether different, instead of the pigment-cells existing in their bodies receiving an additional amount of coloring matter, the cold climate, in a long period of time, gradually absorbed and expelled the small quantity from the cells inherited from their primeval origin ; and, after untold ages, the posterity of the original Red man gradually, through the slow but steady action of natural causes, changes into White, originating a new type with power to transmit a white complexion to their posterity. " I believe," says Dr. Draper, " that the coloration of the skin, whatever the particular tint may be, tawny, yellow, olive, red, or black, is connected with the manner in which the liver is discharging its functions."

*From the Norfolk (Va.) Day-Book.*

"There are a dozen negroes in this city who are slowly turning white, to say nothing of one old fellow who took the start several years ago, and is now completely white. It is curious to watch the progress of these physiological phenomena, which, so far as we are informed, are puzzles to the most astute physiologists. It takes many years for the change to pass entirely over the person, and while it is so passing, the subject presents the most singular, and, in many cases, revolting spectacle imaginable.

"There is one negro man in this city bearing the unmistakable features of the African, whose body is white, and whose face is black as lamp-black—not one of the usual shade of bacon rind, but as black as if he had been painted with a coat of lamp-black. There is a woman whose face is piebald, and another who has lately commenced to turn ; in this last case the first indication

### Mexico.

MONTEZUMA, II. Mexican Emperor of that name; was on the throne in 1519, when Cortez made the invasion, and receiving a wound while a captive under the Spaniards. Died in 1520. Likeness taken by the author from the original painting at Madrid.

### North America.

MANDAN CHIEF.—It was with this tribe the celebrated Indian historian Catline spent much of his time. Tribe now extinct.

### North America.

BLACK HAWK, Indian chief and commander of their forces in their war against the United States, in 1833, holding Gen. Atkinson at bay with 300 warriors against double the number of U. S. troops.

### North America.

MANDAN GIRL, as painted from life by Mr. Catline.

### Arctic Region.

ESQUIMAUX MAN, of Prince Regent Bay, 76 N. lat.—In the region inhabited by this race winters are nine months long.

### Arctic Region.

ESQUIMAUX WOMAN, of Jacobs Bite.—This tribe lives in a region where in winter whiskey freezes as hard as granite.

of a change in complexion was given by the appearance of a white spot behind one of her ears. There is another subject in this city whose face, hands, and arms are white, and whose body is black. The change in this case has been very slow, he having commenced to turn when a boy. It is a remarkable fact that in most cases of this kind the subjects bear on their physiognomies all the features of the full-blooded African.

"Mr. John Pratt, who resides on a farm near Blackiston's Cross Roads, Kent county, Maryland, has a negro man in his employ, whose skin, from his neck to his waist, is turning white. The process has been going on for about three years. He is said to present a very strange appearance."

If such great change has taken place within two hundred and fifty years, the length of time since the first cargo of slaves was landed at the mouth of James river, Virginia, what might be expected a thousand years hence?

Dr. Prichard remarks, that the coloring principle is evidently of a common nature in the skin and hair. The crisped or curly hair of the Negro externally has the appearance of wool, but the microscope shows that it does not differ in its structure from the hair of the fairer races, only in the quantity of pigmentary matter contained in its interior. Wool falls off in mass, and leaves the animal bare, while hair falls off singly and from time to time ; wool is influenced in regard to thickness by the season, being thickest in summer and smallest in winter ; while hair is of uniform thickness.

Dr. Prichard truly observes, even if the hair of the negro were really wool (which it is not), it would not prove him to be of a separate stock, for there are breeds of domesticated animals which have wool, while others of the same species, under different climatical influences, are covered with hair. In fact, all scientific investigation is tending to prove, that the coloring principle in the human body is of a common nature, not only for the skin and hair, but also for the eyes. What greater contrast could there be than between the blonde

4

Jew of Eastern Germany, and the black Arab of the banks of the Jordan, both now known to be of the same origin. Or between the brown Jew of Cochin China or the Great Desert. Or between the brown Afghans of East Afghanistan and the light Afghans of the West, with blue eyes and red hair; between the dark Hindoos of the Dekkan, Malabar, and Ceylon, and the blonde Hindoos of the Himalaya, the olive and blonde Arabs of Armenia and Syria and the brown of Yemen and the black of Jordan? Among Chinese, Siamese, and Japanese, are frequently seen persons of unmixed native blood, says Perthes, who perfectly resemble Europeans in features and complexion. And blue and brown eyes, light hair and complexion, are occasionally seen in all races, even, says Waiz, among the blacks, and in such remote regions that there could be no cause for suspicion of mixture of blood.

Science having exhausted all resources in investigating the living man, has extended its researches to the narrow mansions of the dead. The graves of about every distinct people have been desecrated in order to procure skulls for scientific investigation. But Prof. M. J. Weber says the investigation has only gone to show that there is no proper mark of a definite race-form of the cranium so firmly attached that it may not be found in some other race. And Ziedemann has met with Germans whose skulls have all the characteristics of the Negro race. And Dr. Meigs, after investigating one thousand one hundred and twenty-five different human skulls, says there is a marked tendency of these forms to graduate into one another, more or less insensibly, and none of them can be traced as exclusively belonging to any race or tribe.

## And Prof. Huxley remarks, that cranial measurement affords no indication of race.

"The negro is not the 'missing link' between men and monkeys; he is further removed from anthropoid apes in many respects than the English are. For instance, he has woolly hair, and no monkeys are so ornamented, except, perhaps, a few scarce species in South America. The spur heel of a negro has been spoken of to his disadvantage; but it is doubtful whether his heel projects more than an Englishman's, and that it is not an indentation of the part above the heel, which sometimes gives the appearance of unnatural projection of the latter. Many foolish things are said by opponents of the negro, who frequently quote as a fact what has often been refuted, that the brain of a negro is covered with a black membranous envelope. It is not so. The friends of the negro likewise say foolish things, and argue that England would be all the better for an infusion of negro blood. He did not believe so. One thing is certain, the negro is improvable, because he can now till the ground, smelt iron, and work gold, which he did not do originally. How far he is improvable is a question yet to be solved. It must be remembered, however, that certainly for five or six thousand years, perhaps more, as proved by Egyptian monuments, the negro has lived in Africa much as at present, without in any degree civilizing himself. No nation can elevate itself by condemning another to slavery, and no nation can do its duty to inferior races, or itself attain the highest point of civilization, without trying to raise less favored nations to the highest point they are capable of reaching, be it high or be it low."

"With regard to the brain, Dr. Cadwell remarks, 'In both the Negro and Caucasian races we have the brain, which, except in point of size, is precisely the same in the African as in the European.' The following are the conclusions of Dr. Tiedeman :*—1st. In size, the brain of a Negro is as large as a European. 2d. In regard to the capacity of the cavity, the skull of the Negro in general is not smaller than that of the European and other human races; the opposite opinion is ill-founded, and altogether refuted by my researches. 3d. In the form and structure of the well-possessed spinal chord, the Negro accords in every way with the European, and shows no difference except that arising from the different size of the body. 4th. The cerebellum of the Negro, in regard to its outward form, fissures, and lobes, is exactly similar to that of the European. 5th. The cerebrum has, for the most part, the same form as that of the European. 6th. The brain, in internal structure, is composed of the same substance. 7th. The brain of the Negro is not smaller, compared as to size, nor are the nerves thicker. 8th. The analogy of the brain of the Negro to the Orang-outang is not greater than that of other races, 'except it be in the greater symmetry of the *gyri and sulci; which I very much doubt.*'

"As these features of the brain indicate the degree of intellect and faculties of the mind, we must conclude that no innate difference in the intellectual faculties can be admitted to exist between the Negro and European races. The opposite conclusion is founded on the very facts which have been sufficient to secure the degradation of this race. 'The more interior and natural the Negroes are found in Africa, they are superior in character, in arts, in habits, and in manners, and possess towns, and literature to some extent. Whatever, therefore,' says Robinson, 'may be their tints, their souls are still the same.'

* On the Brain of the Negro; Philosophical Trans., 1838, p. 498.

"It is the opinion of Dr. Prichard, also, that there is nothing whatever in the organization of the brain of the Negro which affords a presumption of inferior endowment, of intellectual or moral faculties. This writer has also given the weight of several skulls of nearly the same size, from which it would appear that there is little constant difference.* The average weight of the brain of a European is about 44 ounces troy weight. Dupuytren's brain weighed 64 ounces : Cuvier's, 63 ounces : Abercrombie's, 63 ounces : the brain of the celebrated Dr. Chalmers only reached 53 ounces ; he had a large head.

"Some other peculiarities might be noticed, such as the articulation of the head with the spine ; the teeth are all of one length, and arranged in a uniform unbroken series. In the Simiæ, whose masticatory apparatus most nearly resembles man, the cuspidati are longer, often very much longer, than the other teeth, and there are intervals in the series of each jaw to receive the cuspidati of the other.

"The lower jaw of man is distinguished by the prominence of the chin, a necessary consequence of the inferior incisors being perpendicular ; by its shortness, and by the oblong convexity and obliquity of the condyles. This remarkable feature in the face of our species is found in no animal. In the Orang-outang it appears as though the part were cut away.

"There yet remains the grand distinction between all the races of man and other animals—

"LANGUAGE ! the miracle of human nature ! The lower animals can indeed communicate with each other by sounds and signs, but they cannot speak. The language of man is the product of art ; animals derive their sounds from nature. Every human language is derived from imitation, and is intelligible only to those who either inhabit the country where it is vernacular, or have been taught it by a master or by books. Homer and Hesiod distinguished man by the title of μερο↓, or *voice-dividing* ; and Aristotle says, ' *Speech* is made to indicate what is expedient and what is inexpedient ; and, in consequence of this, what is just and what is unjust. It is therefore given to men, because it is peculiar to them that of good and evil, of just and unjust, they only, with respect to other animals, possess a sense or feeling.' The existence of language, therefore, says an American writer,† is in itself a proof of the specific character of humanity in all those among whom it is found. The distinguishing characteristics of man, and the peculiar eminence of his nature and his destiny, as these are universally felt and acknowledged by mankind, are usually defined to consist in reason and the faculty of speech. Frederick Von Schlegel has, however, suggested that the peculiar pre-eminence of man consists in this,—that to him alone, among all other of earth's creatures, the ' WORD' has been imparted and communicated. ' The *word*,' he continues, 'actually delivered, and really communicated, is not a mere dead faculty, but an historical reality and occurrence. In the idea of the word considered as the basis of man's dignity

---

* Table exhibiting the weight of several skulls, nearly of the same size,

| | lbs. | oz. | | lbs. | oz. |
|---|---|---|---|---|---|
| Skull of a Greek | 1 | 11¼ | Skull of a Negro, 4, (from Congo) | 1 | 11¼ |
| Skull of a Mulatto | 2 | 10 | Skull of a New Zealander | 1 | 10¾ |
| Skull of a Negro, 1 | 2 | 0 | Skull of a Chinese | 1 | 7¼ |
| Skull of a Negro, 2 | 1 | 12½ | Skull of a Gipsy, without lower jaw | 1 | 13½ |
| Skull of a Negro, 3 | 1 | 5¼ | Skull of a Gipsy, with lower jaw | 2 | 0 |

From the researches of Professor Tiedeman it appears that the average weight of the European brain is from 3 lbs. 3 oz., Troy weight, to 4 lbs.

† Unity of the Human Races, by the Rev. T. Smyth, D. D.

### Alaska.

SITKA INDIAN.—This tribe lives on the coast. Picture furnished to the author by Charles Bryant, sent by the U. S. government to examine and report on the condition of things in our newly acquired territory.

### Alaska.

ALEUTIAN GIRL, 8 years old.—This tribe resides on a group of islands in the North Pacific Ocean. The Otter and Fox skins, furnished to traders, is their chief means of support. The number of the tribe is about 8,700. The picture was furnished the author by Mr. Bryant.

(See letter on another page of this book.)

### South America.

CHARRUAS CHIEF.—The men of this tribe were untamable warriors, averse to agriculture and the arts of civilization, wandering over the arid plains, living under tents of skins or in the forests of Chaco under huts of straw, resisting the Spaniards, and by them at last exterminated. The tribes of the Guaranies, Tobayas, and Payagunses, now occupy their ancient hunting grounds.

### South America.

PATAGONIAN MAN.—This people and their country were first made known to the civilized world by Magellan in 1519. It lies on both sides of the Andes, and contains about 350,000 square miles. The East side only is inhabited. The natives are excellent horsemen, performing extraordinary feats of dexterity on horseback. The males are large and strong, and many of them over 6 feet in height.

### Fejee Islands.

A MALE NATIVE OF THESE ISLANDS.—There are 154 islands in the group, 65 of which are inhabited. They lie in the South Pacific Ocean, and form a portion of Melanesia. These islands are remarkably fertile and now under British rule. Infanticide and Cannibalism have heretofore been extensively practiced by the natives. They are ruled by chiefs, who, in turn, are ruled by the great chief of Ambow, who styles himself king of the Fejeeans.

### Sandwich Islands.

SANDWICH ISLANDER.—Capt. Cook named them after the Earl of Sandwich. About eight of the group are inhabited and extend about 400 miles in a curved line. Population about 150,000. They lie about 2,000 miles from Mexico, 5,000 from China, and 2,700 from the Society Islands on the South. Form of government, a monarchy, limited by a legislative Assembly.

and peculiar destination, *the word is not a mere faculty of speech*, but the fertile root, whence this stately trunk of all language has sprung.' *

"Man may, therefore, be said to differ from every other animal, whatever the family in which he is classed and the color of his skin :—

"*a*. In his feeble and long infancy, late puberty, and slow growth.

"*b*. In possessing the power of SPEECH ; holding communion with his fellow-men by words.

"*c*. Smoothness of skin ; no natural weapons of offence or defence.

"*d*. In the general conformation of the body ; the structure of the pelvis, thighs, and legs ; the incurvation of the sacrum and os coccygis.

"*e*. The erect posture ; the adaptation of certain muscles to that state ; the peculiar structure of the feet ; the position of the eyes ; the possession of two hands, beautifully and perfectly constructed ; and in the great strength of the thumb, in comparison with the monkey race.

"*f*. Large proportion of the cerebral cavity to the face, and the size and weight of the brain in relation to the nerves which spring from it.

"*g*. In having teeth all of the same length ; the inferior incisors being approximated.

"*h*. No intermaxillary bone ; shortness of the lower jaw.

"*i*. In the shape of the head ; the situation of the foramen magnum, and the articulation of the skull with the spinal column, by the middle of its basis, and the absence of the ligamentum nuchæ.

"*j*. Great development of the cerebral hemispheres, and the greater number of mental faculties, intellectual and moral."

Perhaps it is well, in closing this part of our subject, to state, that the most widely different among mankind have the same periods of gestation, of infancy, of puberty, of maturity and longevity, and are subject to the same diseases ; and the result of their union is invariably a fertile offspring. The Jewish Scriptures positively assert that the reason why Adam, after the fall, called his wife Eve, was because she was the mother of all living. As Dr. Kennicott translates : Because he found she was *still* to be the mother of all living. Or, as the *Chaldee* better translates the passage : The mother of all the sons of men. Or the *Arabic* version : Because she was to be the mother of every rational living animal. In the ninth chapter of Genesis we find : And God said unto Noah, This is the token of the covenant, which I have established

* The Philosophy of History (Bohn's edition).

between me and *all flesh* that is upon the earth, and the sons of Noah that went forth of the ark were Shem and Ham and Japheth. These are the sons of Noah, and of them was the whole earth overspread. These quotations show that God proclaimed, through the Jewish Scriptures, that Eve was the mother of all the sons of men. From Genesis, ninth chapter, fourth verse, we learn that the *Blood is the life;* and *Harvey* and *Hunter* have both clearly demonstrated that the blood of man is the life, as it is the first principle that lives and last that dies, and from it every fluid and every solid of the human frame are derived. And we find the same Almighty truth reiterated under the Gospel dispensation, by Paul, in his powerful appeal to the Athenians, where, after preaching to the idolatrous worshippers the God that made the world and all things therein, he adds : " And hath made of ONE BLOOD (*i. e.* one life\*) all nations of men for to dwell on all the face of the earth, and hath determined the times before appointed, and the bounds of their habitation. Acts, xvii. 26.

\* Adam only was created from the dust of the ground, and it was into his nostrils only the Almighty breathed life.

Eve was made from a rib taken from Adam's side, not from the dirt of the ground, and no account is given in the sacred text of breathing into her nostrils the breath of life. Then, truly, we can say, from one life (*i. e.* Blood) hath all mankind descended.

# PART SECOND.

IT is a well established fact, that civilization had its origin with the primeval or red families of mankind. The three great nations of antiquity, India, China, and Egypt, were the first to organize regular governments, and establish set forms for religious worship ; and the brilliancy of their achievements remain undimmed by the lustre of the present hour. Chinese history reaches back 2,637 B. C. The records of India are older than Moses : while Egypt, far back in the dim ages of antiquity, with its blazing civilization, looms up like a meteor in the night of time. Some philosophers contend that man rose by his own exertions from a savage to a civilized state. One of them says : When they first crept forth from the newly-formed earth, a dumb and filthy herd, they fought for acorns and lurking-places with their nails and fists, then with clubs, and at last with arms, which, taught by experience, they had forged. They then invented names for things, and words to express their thoughts. After which they began to desist from war, to fortify cities, and enact laws. But investigation and reflection have satisfied us that it was not so. Because all nations and tribes have a tradition referring back to a time when some one or more of their ancestors received instructions or were miraculously preserved by the interposition of the gods. These faint impressions and feebly retained tradi-

tions in the mind of man, show how sensitive and con-
scious he is of a fallen condition.   Abraham himself knew
little of civilization when he first entered Egypt to procure *corn*.   Here he beheld how industry, parent of
enjoyment, had gathered the luxuries of all climes.   The
richly cultivated fields, the gorgeous palaces seen at Memphis, must have surpassed the brightest dreams of his
youth.   And what must have been his amazement when
first beholding the mighty pyramids of Gheezeh with
Shoopho's lofty summit, and its twenty-four companions,
all standing within a few miles of Memphis ; and the
youngest of these mighty monuments had been erected
over four hundred years before he was born.

The reader must not think the great antiquity I
have attributed to Egyptian monuments comes in contact
with the Bible.   It is an important fact that no one of
the inspired writers of that book pretend to give a chronology of the age of the world.   The author of the Book
of Genesis says, " In the beginning God created the
heaven and the earth," but he does not say when that
beginning was.   Now, what no one of the inspired
writers attempted, Archbishop Usher, a learned divine
of Armagh, Ireland (who died in 1656), undertook to
accomplish.   He invented a chronology by which he
attempted to give the precise date when each and all the
great events recorded in the inspired volume took place.
His computations were adopted by the English Epis-
copal Church, and confirmed by Act of the English
Parliament, and are found at the head of the columns
containing the marginal notes.   The Protestant churches
have, I believe, generally adopted his chronology, but no
one supposes that because they are found in the Bible,

and sanctioned by Act of the English Parliament, makes
them inspired. Above three hundred persons have made
Biblical computations concerning the age of the world,
each one differing from all the rest. We might adopt
the tables of Alphonsus the Tenth, which that king compiled at an expense of four hundred thousand crowns,
making the world, B. C. 6,984 years old. Or that of
Rabbi Lipman's Computations, making it only B. C.
3,616. Then we have what is called the Septuagint
chronology, which gives 3,246 years from the Deluge to
Christ, and 5,872 from Adam to Christ. Ptolemy Philadelphus, after he had liberated one hundred thousand
Jews from bondage, requested the High Priest of Israel
to send him a faithful copy of the Jewish Law, which
the High Priest had written on parchment, in letters of
gold, and sent as requested. After which the king employed seventy-two learned men, who assembled at the
Isle of Pharos, Alexandria, 240 B. C., and translated the
Hebrew Scriptures into the Greek language. The trans-
lators were shut up in thirty-six cells, each pair translated
the whole, and on comparing the thirty-six copies, JUSTIN
MARTYR affirms they did not vary a word. This translation took place before the corruption of the Hebrew
Bible by the Jews, to throw early prophecies concerning
the Messiah out of date. These alterations were done
in the time of Seder Alam Rabbi, one hundred and thirty
years after Christ, yet it is this computation, thus altered
by the Jews, that has been followed by Bishop Usher,
which appears in all our English Bibles, sanctified by act
of Parliament. This uninspired Parliamentary blunder,
added to that of the Council of Trent in 1546, has been
converted into a geological weapon which *Voltaire, Hig-*

gins, *Dolbach, Hume, Bolingbroke, Paine, Rousseau, Hobbs, Gibbon, Volney,* and other infidel writers have used to destroy confidence in the Divinity of God's word. Josephus, the Jewish author, who wrote his history at. Rome, immediately after the fall of Jerusalem, very nearly agrees with the Septuagint, making the world 5,759 years old at the birth of Christ, and giving 3,146 from Christ to the deluge, making a difference of only one hundred years.

Now, Usher makes the world only 4,004 years old at the birth of the Saviour (Latin version, Catholic, the same), and allows only 2,348 years to have intervened between Him and the deluge, which is 902 years less than the Septuagint, and cuts from the age of the world 1,868 years, and near 3,000 years from the computation of Alphonsus. The age of the world, we believe, is known only to its Maker, and as he did not deem it necessary or expedient to reveal it during the ages of inspiration, it most likely will forever remain a mystery. Neither do we believe that any chronological table has yet been invented (Bishop Usher's included) that comes within five thousand years of giving the correct date of the flood. The evidence gathered from monumental history and tradition in Egypt, China, and India, with past geological researches, demand, for truth's sake, the adoption of a new and more extended chronology. If it had not been for the barbarous fanaticism of numerous nations, and all creeds, we might have been able to arrive at its correct date. As it is not from the Jews only we receive light; for among all nations we find vague traditions of that mighty event.

The Egyptians, says *Diodorus Siculus,* had a tradition of the destruction of the whole living world in its primordial times by a Deluge. DEUCALION, who by advice of the Creator built an ark, by it saved himself and his wife, and through them the human race was renewed.

*The Greeks* had the same tradition, only confining the Deluge to Greece : see *Apollodorus. Berosus*, a writer who lived at the period of the Macedonian dynasties, in his second book, states that the Chaldeans had an account of a flood which HE compiled from written documents kept at Babylon.

*Phenicians*, according to Hieronymus, an Egyptian writer, had a tradition of it at Joppa. *The Chou King*, the History of China, written by *Confucius*, opens with an account of a flood ; and *Tao See*, a leader of an opposing school of philosophy, speaks of the Deluge occurring in the reign of Niuhoa : he states the seasons were then changed, day and night confounded, great waters overspread the universe, and men were reduced to the condition of fishes.

*Hindoos* have an extended account of a flood in one of their sacred poems (*Mahahharat*). *Mohammed* has the old Arabian account of it in the Koran : also in *Africa* among the blacks ; and in Mexico, North and South America, before the discovery by Columbus, all had a tradition of the deluge. And Humboldt appropriately remarks that similar traditions exist among all the nations of the earth, and like the relics of a vast shipwreck, are highly interesting in the philosophical study of our species.

But the loss, from the destruction of ancient archives in Asia Minor, Greece, and Syria, and in almost every part of the globe, can never be replaced. In defence of the arsenal, Julius Cæsar could not prevent the destruction of the great Ptolemaic library (by conflagration) from the furious attacks of the Alexandrian populace. While the subsequent ruthless decree of *Omar* enforced the obliteration of the Christian Bibliothecal Repository at Alexandria (seventy thousand volumes), which it had taken six hundred years to accumulate. The Tartar conquerors in China, devoted to the flames the precious annals of ancient history, while their brethren destroyed nearly all Indian and Asiatic libraries. In the Saracenic torrent that overthrew the dynasty of Chosroes, Khuzruff destroyed all the volumes which for ages had accumulated in the Persian archives. Did not the Syrian annals perish with the fleets and fortress of Phenicia, when Alexandria overthrew the mistress of the deep? And did not Marius destroy the chronicles at Carthage? And in the fall of Hierosolima, was not Titus amenable for the destruction of the Hebrew archives? And did not Brennus, the Gaul, destroy the seven-hilled city, with all her public records, 390 B. C.? And we must not forget the misdirected zeal and monkish fanaticism that marked every Christian country—Polimpsesting everywhere what they called heathen manuscripts and monumental inscriptions. All authorities contemporary with the decline of Pharaonic glory, agree that there were in Egypt over twenty thousand volumes, the productions of Suphis, Athothis, Necho, and Petosisis, all Egyptian Pharaohs, besides thousands of other books, the productions of Priests, Physicians, and Philosophers, which were all annihilated by the Persian invasion 525 B. C., and thus the paper records of Egypt were blotted out.

It was by consulting these numerous ancient works of the Egyptian poets and philosophers, which had for thousands of years been accumulating in the richly stored libraries of Heliopolis and Memphis, that Moses became learned in all the wisdom of the Egyptians, and became so mighty in words and in deeds. Acts, vii. 22.

But notwithstanding this wholesale destruction of ancient manuscripts, there yet remained, along the banks of the Nile, carved in stones, an imperishable record of Egypt's great antiquity.

Herodotus, a Grecian and native of Halicarnassus, visited Egypt 430 B. C., and 95 years after the Persian invasion. One hundred and seventy years after Herodotus, who is called the Father of History, Manetho, High Priest and sacred scribe of Heliopolis, and a native of the Solemnitic nome in the eastern delta, Lower Egypt, at the command of the Persian king Ptolemy Philadelphus, then reigning in Egypt, compiled a history of Egypt from the earliest times, down to the Alexandrian invasion, 332 B. C. Manetho was a very learned man, having received his education in the same town where Moses had been educated, about 1,000 years before. He wrote his history in the Greek language, about 260 B. C. Sixty years after him, Eratosthenes of Cyrene, Grammarian, Mathematician, Astronomer, Geographer, and Librarian, compiled his Laterculus, or catalogue of Egyptian kings. Then we have Diodorus, another Greek, who wrote about 40 B. C. Neither Diodorus nor Herodotus understood, or even comprehended the hieroglyphical language of Egypt. After that we have Josephus, Julius Africanus, Eusebius. Then later, Tacitus, Plutarch, Pausanias, Pliny, and a host of others. The only reliable writer on Egypt, among all I have quoted, was Manetho, and his writings perished the first century after Christ.

For ages the crumbling ruins of its mighty monuments, its gorgeous temples, and tombs, and magnificent sculpture, have filled the world with astonishment and admiration ; for above two thousand years the Persian, the Greek, the Roman, and Mohammedan conquerors used it as a stake in the game of empire.

While Providence permitted these barbarian monarchs to conquer and subdue its degenerate inhabitants, although monuments, temples, tombs, sculpture, and stones were everywhere carved with hieroglyphics, inviting them to read, their eyes continued closed, and their understandings darkened, utterly unable to comprehend its intellectual greatness.

But, in the 17th century, a new spirit of inquiry revived, which led Paul, Lucas, Shaw, Volney, Savary, Norden, Rossini, Peacock, Mallet, Bruce, and others, to visit the shores of the Nile. But Turkish fanaticism stood much in the way of European explorers. It was at this interesting time, Bonaparte, that child of destiny, left the shores of France at the head of that great expedition, with a view of establishing an Oriental empire, wherein the children of the Frank and Gaul would hold supremacy over the Northeastern provinces of Asia and Africa, equal to that which has been established in the Eastern Hemisphere by the Anglo-Saxon race. But fate threw obstacles in the way, which turned the energy of its commander into European channels. But Napoleon was a lover of science and the arts, and it was here, amidst the roar of artillery, and martial music of his camps, he directed the savans of France that accompanied the expedition to scrutinize the monuments of Egypt. It had been overrun by different conquerors for above 2,000 years, yet its intellectual treasures remained undiscovered. Yes, from Napoleon's advent into Egypt, ages slumbering in the womb of time, and generations yet unborn, will yet enjoy the effulgence of that light of which, in our day, only gleams have reached the world. While in 1800 he opened the way to the long lost history of Egypt, on the 30th of April, 1803, after his return to Paris,. he made to this Government, through Livingston and Monroe, the princely donation of Louisiana.

Thus, while the world of civilized man was benefited by his advent into Egypt, America should ever remember the time when he presented the greatest river on the planet and over one hundred million square miles of territory to the United States, with the satirical political prophecy, " I have just given to England a maritime rival that will, sooner or later, humble her pride."

The result of the French savan's explorations in Egypt, was published by order of the government of France. Then came Belzoni, who entered and explored a pyramid at Memphis, still known by his name. He also made additional explorations at Thebes. Then came the Rosetta-stone, discovered by Mons. Bouchard, a French officer of engineers. Then in 1819, Dr. Young, the Scotchman, published what he supposed to be the key, but in his hands it would not unlock the door. Champollion appeared, in 1822, with an article on hieroglyphic writing, which he read to the Royal Academy of Belles Lettres in Paris. Information was now on the increase, and the French government, in 1828, fitted out another expedition, headed by Champollion, to make additional explorations. At the same time the Grand Duke of Tuscany, prompted by scientific inquiry, sent Prof. Rosellini, and four Italian

artists.   These two expeditions, sent by France and Tuscany, were blended into one, and reached Egypt on the
same vessel.   They all returned in 1829, with the richest
archæological spoils that ever left Egypt.  Champollion's
part was to illustrate the historical monuments and the
grammar of the hieroglyphical language of Egypt, while
Rosellini was to elucidate, by the civil monuments, the
manners and customs of the ancient people, and the com-
pilation of a hieroglyphical dictionary.  Champollion finding his end approaching, finished his grammar on his
death-bed, and placing the manuscript in charge of a few
friends that surrounded him, requested them to preserve it
carefully, remarking, " I hope it will be my visiting-card to
posterity."

The French Government published his works, while
Rosellini in 1832 issued the first volume of his Monuments of Egypt and Nubia, and announced he would
finish in ten volumes of text and four hundred plates, the
Civil and Religious, Military and Monumental History
of Egypt.   Thus, while France and Tuscany were fostering a new school of Egyptian literature, many private
individuals in Great Britain, at great personal expense,
continued to prosecute inquiry.   Among the most energetic and reliable were Sir J. Gardner, Wilkinson, and
Samuel Birch.   Humboldt, the great naturalist, became
highly interested in the wonderful developments now going on in Egyptian chronology, and proposed to the king
of Prussia the importance of sending an exploring party
to the banks of the Nile, and suggested Dr. Lepsius as a
suitable person to take charge of the expedition.   The
king acquiesced, and the expedition was immediately fitted
out, and a large sum placed in the hands of Dr. Lepsius,

### Pius IX.,

POPE.—Born May 13th, 1792; elected Pope June 16th, 1846, and coronated June 21st, 1846.    Population of the State of the Church, 723,121; religion, Catholic.    He is supposed to be the spiritual head of about 300,000,000 of people.

### Napoleon III.,

EMPEROR OF FRANCE.—Born April 20th, 1808; elected for President December 20th, 1848; proclaimed Emperor December 2d, 1852. Population of his empire, 40,968,310; religion, Catholic; form of government, Military Imperialism.

### Francis Joseph,

EMPEROR OF AUSTRIA.—Born August 18th, 1830; ascended the throne December 2d, 1848.  Population of his empire, 35,553,000; religion, Catholic.

### Isabelle II.,

Formerly QUEEN OF SPAIN.—Born October 10th, 1830; succeeded her father September 29th, 1833; proclaimed Queen at Madrid, October 2d, 1833; abdicated and fled to France September 30th, 1868, and now, April 1870, is still an exile, and her ancient kingdom yet struggles in the throes of revolution.  Population, 16,302,625; religion, Catholic.

### Louis,

KING OF PORTUGAL.—Born October 31st, 1838; ascended the throne November 11th, 1861.  Population of his kingdom, 4,347,441; religion, Catholic.

### Victor Emanuel,

KING OF ITALY.—Born March 14th, 1820; succeeded his father as king of Sardinia July 28th, 1849, and received the title of king of Italy March 17th, 1861.  Population of his kingdom, 25,404,773; religion, Catholic.

who, with the aid of seven scientific men, started to
retrace the steps of his numerous predecessors over the
sacred ground hallowed by countless generations of antiquity. In the mean time our own country was being represented by Prof. Gliddon and Dr. Morton, of Philadelphia.

Now the result of the investigation in regard to the
age of the pyramids, Humboldt remarks, man yet pos-
sesses authoritative portraits of kings, as far back as the
fourth dynasty of Manetho. This dynasty embraces the
constructors of the great pyramids of Geezeh, Cophen,
Cheops, and Menkeso, commencing 3,400 years B. C.
This is 154 years before the Septuagint flood, and 1052
years before the time of Bishop Usher's deluge.

Now, there are 31 dynasties of Egyptian Pharaohs,
which will average near 150 years to each dynasty. Rosellini carries the 16th dynasty up to 2,272 B. C. Then
there are 15 dynasties yet, beyond which, at the same
rate, would fix the period for the commencing of the first
dynasty at above 4,000 B. C. Dr. Lepsius places the
reign of the first king of Egypt to commence 3,893 B. C.,
which is 1550 years before the deluge, according to Usher.
And Bunsen dates the advent of Menes, founder of the
United Kingdom of Egypt, at 3,623 B. C.

Bishop Rasle remarks, that it was an old country in
the infant age of Greece. The first dynasty of Egypt
was founded 2,666 years before Nineveh and Babylon ;
2,393 years before Moses began to write the Bible ; above
2,000 years before the appearance of the sacred books or
monumental inscriptions in India ; 750 years before the
deluge, as fixed by the Septuagint Bible ; 1555 years before the deluge, according to Usher ; and 1893 years

before Abraham was born. Crozier's history of China, 15 quarto volumes, translated by Imperial authority, dates the commencement of the Chinese government 2,953 B. C., while Dr. Lepsius has discovered monumental evidence, proving that the government of Egypt had passed from priestly jurisdiction into the hands of Menes, its first king, one thousand years before the Chinese were a people.

Through Philology, we learn there are about three thousand different dialects—587 in Europe, 937 in Asia, 226 in Africa, and 1,264 in America. Of course, only a very few of this number have an alphabet, or means of communicating thoughts, except by voice. Some may have rude drawings by which they represent ideas and sound, but without instruction how to abbreviate or reduce them into current written characters.

The alphabets of different nations contain the following letters :

| | | | |
|---|---|---|---|
| English 26. | French 23. | Italian 20. | Spanish 27. |
| German 26. | Slavonic 27. | Russian 41. | Latin 22. |
| Greek 24. | Hebrew 22. | Arabic 28. | Persian 32. |
| Sanscrit 52. | Chinese 214. | | |

There are twenty thousand words in Spanish, twenty-five thousand in Latin, from twenty-two to twenty-five thousand in English, thirty thousand in French, forty-five thousand in Italian, fifty thousand in Greek, and eighty thousand in German.

Various plans have been suggested how and when writing was first discovered. Many persons have contended that the Jews received it from God, and that the Hebrew was the first written language, and the Bible the first book. The transit from spoken to written language appears to be of indefinite antiquity, up to the days of Champollion, 1825. The invention of writing had been traced to the Hebrews, Phœnicians, Chaldeans, Chinese, Hindoos, and Egyptians, while the great mass of the Christian world believed it originated with Moses, and that the tables of stone contained the first writing ever given to man.

But this view of the subject does not accord with the sacred volume; for in the fifth chapter of Genesis, first verse: " This is the book of the generation of Adam." Here reference is made to the book of the genealogy. And the Hebrews had other sacred books not included in the Bible. One called the Wars of Jehovah, from which a quotation is given in the Bible, Numbers, 21st chap., 14th verse. Learned theologians admit the Book of Job is not a Hebrew production, although accepted and authenticated by the Jewish lawgiver. Job lived in the land of Uz, Armenia, of which Edom was a district. The country is known by us as Arabia. Job was an Arabian, probably of the Joctan race, and according to Hales, his probable epoch was about 2,337 b. c., or 800 years before Moses. One of Job's friends was named Eliphaz, the Temanite. Now in the 36th chapter of Genesis, 4th to 10th, and in 1st Chronicles, 1st chapter, 35th verse, we learn that Eliphaz was Esau's oldest son ; there, and in the Book of Job, are the only places in the Bible where Eliphaz is named. Being called a Temanite, Jeremiah, 49th chapter, 7th to 20th, makes Teman a province of Edom. Job remarks, "Oh that my words were now written ! Oh that they were printed in a book." He also expresses a desire that his adversary had written a book.

Thus it is proven that writing and books were known among the Gentiles eight hundred years before Moses' day, and the pure belief of one God not limited to the Jewish patriarch Abraham after the flood. Last of all, if the Hebrew had been the language of Heaven, the *Saviour* would never have abandoned it while expiring on the Cross. " *Eli, Eli,* lama sabachthani?" is not Hebrew, but Armenian.

Ancient opinions of some of the great heathen masters concerning God :

"Zoroaster asserts that the first uncreated cause perfected all things, and then transferred them over to the government of a second mind ; which second mind or power, mankind being ignorant of the paternal, generally invested them with the attributes of divinity, and worshipped them as the first God.

"Chinese books are full of descriptions of the first Heaven, and declare that mankind will be happy in that attractive abode, where all things grow without labor, where no war of the elements or inclement air shall ever come."

*From the Sacred Book of India.*

[One hundred and twenty-ninth book of the Rig Veda—Translated from the Sanscrit, by Max Müller.]

" In judging it, we should bear in mind that it was not written by a gnostic or by a pantheistic philosopher, but by a poet who felt all these doubts and problems as his own, without any wish to convince or to startle, only uttering what had been weighing on his mind, just as later poets would sing the doubts and sorrows of their heart.

"Nor Aught nor Naught existed ; yon bright sky
Was not, nor heaven's broad woof outstretched above.
What covered all ? what sheltered ? what concealed ?
Was it the water's fathomless abyss ?
There was not death—yet was there naught immortal.
There was no confine betwixt day and night ;
The only One breathed breathless by itself,
Other than It there nothing since has been.
Darkness there was, and all at first was veiled
In gloom profound—an ocean without light—
The germ that still lay covered in the husk
Burst forth, one nature, from the fervent heat.
Then first came love upon it, the new spring
Of mind—yea, poets in their hearts discerned,
Pondering, this bond between created things
And uncreated. Comes this spark from earth.

Piercing and all-pervading, or from heaven?
Then seeds were sown, and mighty powers arose—
Nature below, and power and will above—
Who knows the secret? who proclaimed it here,
Whence, whence this manifold creation sprang?
The gods themselves came later into being—
Who knows from whence this great creation sprang?
He from whom all this great creation came,
Whether his will created or was mute,
The Most High Seer that is in highest heaven,
He knows it—or perchance even He knows not."

After the worship of a Supreme being had been partially discontinued, it is reasonable to suppose that adoration of the heavenly bodies was the next religion that prevailed to a great extent. But the wise men amongst all Heathen nations, almost to a man (except those who denied the being of a God), believed in one great *First Cause—intelligent, self-supporting,* and *Supreme.*

It is a remarkable fact that the three great nations of antiquity, Hindoos, Chinese, and Egyptians, had each, at the very commencement of their annals, a system of writing so complete, that we do not find any improvement in after ages. The Hieroglyphical language found on the early monuments of Egypt was perfect, and was neither altered nor changed down to the closing period of its thirty-one dynasties, 331 B. C.

As the Egyptians have the oldest annals, we must award to them the glory of being either the receivers, inventors, or restorers of Hieroglyphical writing. The Rosetta-stone, dug up near the mouth of the Nile, by Bouchard, a French officer of engineers, while digging the foundation of Fort Julian, is three feet long, twenty-nine inches in breadth, and twelve inches thick, and is now in the British Museum.

It has three inscriptions: *First,* Hieroglyphic; *Sec-*

*ond*, Enchorial writing of the people, termed Demotic ; *Third*, Greek, which purported to be a translation of the other two. The event recorded on this stone was the coronation of Epiphanes, which took place in the month of March, 196 B. C. It is headed : " The year IX. of the son of the sun, Ptolemy ever living beloved of Pthah."

Ptolemy the king, like the Government of the United States, had crushed a rebellion. And part of the inscription on the Rosetta-stone (showing how he treated his subjects, may be of interest to the reader) reads : " I have ordered that the citizens who laid down their rebellious arms, and those whose sentiments had been in times of trouble opposed to the Government, and who had returned to their duty, should be maintained in possession of their property. That having entered Memphis as the avenger of my father and his own rightful crown, I have punished, *as they deserved*, the chiefs of those who revolted against my father, devastated the country, and despoiled the temples."

The discovery of this stone, with a Greek translation of the Hieroglyphical writing of Egypt, gave a new impetus and created new energy in Hieroglyphical students.

Through the mighty genius of Champollion now began to flow the blessings of Napoleon's advent into Egypt. With renewed effort he demonstrated to the Royal Academy in Paris, that the ancient Egyptians had made use of pure Hieroglyphical signs, that is to say, of characters representing the images of material objects to represent simply the sounds of the names of the Greek and Roman sovereigns inserted on the monuments of Dendera, Thebes, Erne, Edfoe, Omlos, and Philoe. The savans of Europe were astounded at this great discovery of Champollion's; he had previously, in 1814, recorded his hope, in his "Egypt under the Pharaohs," that there would at last be discovered upon these tablets, whereon Egypt had but painted material objects, the sounds of language and the expression of thought. His last great work, in 1824, opened the door to Egypt's time-honored chronicles, just when the intellect of Europe was growing weary and doubtful of success. Young, the Scotch savant, had previously published a small volume claiming the honor of discovery, and awarding to Champollion the honor of extending the alphabet. But with the force of an earthquake, Champollion overthrew all the false theories of his predecessors, and with an intellectual hurricane blew from the crumbling ruins the dust of ages which had hid from the Greeks and Romans the glories of Pharaonic Epochs, the deeds of the most civilized, pious, learned, and warlike people of antiquity, whose government exceeded all others, thousands of years in duration, and whose works surpassed in magnitude, boldness of conception, accuracy of execution, and splendor of achievement, anything recorded in the history of man. Champollion appeared to have an intuitive conception, and could arrive at conclusions at a glance, defining the meaning of every obscure legend.

The following extracts we take from Prof. Glidden:

"Drawing, in those early days, was the most effective to satisfy those cravings inherent in intellectual man, which had in view the creation of a power to communicate with persons removed from the draughtsman by time and space, rather than to *imitate* the various works of nature. The study of representing *things* pictorially, had, in those primitive times, no other object than to effect that which was completely achieved by the introduction of *signs* for SOUNDS.

"Of the introduction of these *letters*, we have the fact before us in every Egyptian legend, from the earliest postdiluvian epoch admissible, down to the extinction of *hieroglyphical* writing in the third century of the Christian era, a period of at least 3,006 years; but we cannot name the introducer, except in the legendary THOTH ; nor state positively how this discovery was made in Egypt. —The arts of writing, drawing, painting, and sculpture, in ancient Egypt, were emblematized by one SYMBOL ; and, in hieroglyphics, were expressed thus :

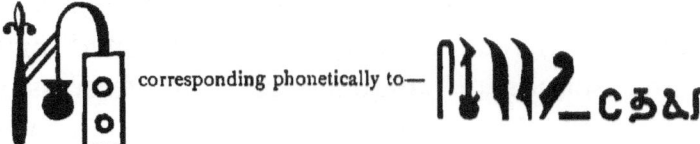

SKHAI. This symbol expressed, in the sacred character, the *signification* and the *sound* of the words 'to paint,' 'the painter,' 'to write,' and 'the writer ;' as also 'writings'—γραμματα. The *symbol* itself is compounded of three things, all connected with its meaning ; as 'the *reed,*' used in writing, at the present day, by the Arabs, and termed 'qâlam ;' 'the vase,' or ink-bottle ; and the 'scribe's palette,' whereon he poured his *red* and *black* inks, filling the little hollows in its centre.

| *Reed.* | *Vase.* | *Palette.* |

"In precisely the same manner, in ancient Greek, the words 'to describe,' 'to draw,' 'to engrave,' and 'to *write,*' were all comprised in the same verb—γραφειν.

"By analogical reasoning, then, we may infer, that the progressive steps toward the development of hieroglyphical writing may have been in the following order :

"1st. That material objects struck their view, and to transmit them to posterity, or to preserve the *idea* of one of these objects, they painted the *figure* of the thing itself; and this would be FIGURATIVE writing.

"2d. That the insufficiency of this plan in application was immediately felt.  In painting the figure of a *man,* they could not express *what* man ; and to define him, they added a *tropical sign* or *symbol* of another thing in some way associated with this particular man.  This would be SYMBOLIC writing.

"3d. That then certain arbitrary, and, in due course, conventional signs were added, to express the *idea* of an immaterial object ; as a HATCHET for a *god,* a URÆUS (asp) for *royalty,* etc.

"4th. They finally contrived to introduce divers representatives of SOUND, taking, to denote each letter, those objects the *names* of which, in their language, began with the *initial sound* of that designation ; that is, when they wanted to denote the articulation L, they drew a *Lion,* and so on. This would be PHONETIC writing ; and is the principle that originated many *Semitic* alphabets, as the Hebrew, the Samaritan, the Phœnician, etc., as well as those of some other nations.

"In Egyptian hieroglyphics, as may be seen in part by the alphabet, there are, in some instances, as many as twenty-five different characters used to represent *one letter,* and these are termed 'homophones' of that letter.

"One immense advantage accrued in *monumental* legends from this variety, for the artist was thus enabled to employ those figures which, while representing the articulated *sound* of the letter, had by their form a relation to the idea these signs were to express.  The writer could thus, by the judicious selection of his letters from the variety of his *homophones*, convey a meaning of admiration, praise, dignity, beauty, strength, etc., or he could denote disgust, hatred, insignificance, or other depreciatory opinions.

"I will endeavor to render this apparent by an example. Suppose we wished to adopt the same system in our language and write the word 'AMERICA' in hieroglyphics. I use pure Egyptian hieroglyphics as letters, adapting them to English values :

A—We might select one out of many more or less appropriate symbols ; as an *asp, apple, altar, amaranth, anchor, archer, arrow, antelope, axe.* I choose the *asp*, symbolic of 'sovereignty.'

M—We have a *mace, mast, mastiff, moon, mouse, mummy, musket, maize.* I select the *mace*, indicative of 'military dominion.'

E—An *ear, egg, eagle, elk, eye.* The *eagle* is undoubtedly the most appropriate, being the 'national arms of the Union,' and means 'courage.

*Asp.*　　*Mace.*　　*Eagle.*　　*Ram.*　　*Infant.*　　*Cake.*　　*Sacred Tau.*

R—A *rabbit, ram, raccoon, ring, rock, rope.* I take the *ram*, by synecdoche, placing a part for the whole, emblematic of 'frontal power'—*intellect*—and sacred to Amun.

I—An *insect, Indian, infant, ivy.* An *infant* will typify 'the juvenile age' and still undeveloped strength of this great country.

C—A *cake, caldron, cat, clam, carman, constellation, curlew, cone, crescent.* The crescent would indicate the rising power of the United States ; the constellation of *stars* would emblematize the States, and is borne aloft in the American banner ; but I choose the *cake*—the *consecrated bread*—typical of a '*civilized* region.'

A—An *anchor*, or any of the above words beginning with *A*, would answer : the *anchor* would symbolize 'maritime greatness,' associated with 'safety' and 'stability ;' but not being an *Egyptian* emblem, I take the 'sacred Taû,' the symbol of 'eternal life,' which in the alphabet is an *A*.

To designate that by this combination of *symbols* we mean a *country*, I add the sign ▬▬▬▬ , in Coptic 'Kah,' meaning a country, and determinative of geographical appellatives. We thus obtain *phonetically*—

A　　M　　E　　R　　I　　C　　A

COUNTRY :

while *symbolically*, the characters chosen imply 'sovereignty, military dominion, courage, intelligence, juvenility, civilization, and eternal durability.'

7

The law of Phonetic Hieroglyphics is, that the picture of a physical object shall give the sign of the sound with which the name begins in the Egyptian tongue.

Thus, Lion is called Labo in Egyptian, the same as L might be the initial for that animal in English. The same in Hebrew, where the Lion is called Labi ; in fact, the letter L is only an abbreviating position of a recumbent Lion.

The Hebrew, Samaritan, Arabic, Phœnician, and other Semitic tongues are all governed by the same principle. In fact, the distinct articulation of Phonetic Hieroglyphics may be resolved into sixteen sounds, represented by sixteen Egyptian letters, with their Hemephones, which are identical to the sixteen Cadmean characters, and they represent the distinct elementary sounds of the human voice, because all alphabetical sounds are more or less compound, and are reducible into their primitive elements. Thus the fact that the Greek and Phœnician alphabets contained at first only sixteen distinct letters is not only established by analogy and historical testimony, but by nature itself. The Greeks and other nations completed the powers of their alphabet by adding other letters to represent compound sounds. The Egyptians without extending their phonetics arrived at the same result, only by another process. It was a strange chronological coincidence that the fifteenth century B. C. witnessed the exodus of the Israelites from Egypt, and their organiza-

### Christian IX.,

KING OF DENMARK.—Born April 8th, 1818; ascended the throne November 15th, 1863. Population, 1,753,787; religion, Protestant.

### Alexander II.,

EMPEROR OF RUSSIA.—Born April 29th, 1818; ascended the throne March 2d, 1855. Population of his empire, 78,400,000; religion, Greek Church. A great military Power; 180,000 young men kept constantly in military schools, 10,000 are educated for officers, while its regular standing army numbers 697,137.

### Victoria,

QUEEN OF ENGLAND.—Born May 24th, 1819; ascended the throne June 20th, 1837; coronated June 28th, 1838. Population of her empire, 191,330,000, about 180,000,000 of which are in India; religion, Protestant.

### Charles,

PRINCE OF ROMANIA.—Proclaimed ruler October 24th, 1866. Population of his kingdom, 4,605,510; religion, Jewish.

### Charles XV.,

KING OF SWEDEN AND NORWAY.—Born May 3d, 1826; ascended the throne July 8th, 1859; coronated at Stockholm May 3d, and at Dronheim August 8th, 1860. Population of his kingdom, 5,874,536, of which two-thirds belong to Sweden; religion, Protestant.

### Leopold II.,

KING OF BELGIUM.—Born April 9th, 1835; ascended the throne December 10th, 1865. One of the youngest states in Europe until the revolt of the Netherlands in the 16th century, Antwerp was the great seaport of Europe, and thousands of vessels crowded its port. Population of his kingdom, 4,897,794; religion, Catholic.

tion into an orderly community by Moses, with the introduction of the Hebrew alphabet ; and the importation of
a primitive alphabet from Phœnicia, by Cadmus (son of
Agenor the king of Phœnicia), into Greece, at a period
when that country was tributary to the Pharaohs and
overrun with their armies. The same century witnessed
the foundation of Thebes, with all its oriental mysteries,
and the emigration of Danaus, the founder of Danai at
Argos, where colossal ruins even to this day point to
their Nilotic origin. We can trace the foundation of
Athens itself to an Egyptian colony led by Cecrops from
Sais ; and it was, says Dunaker, in this century, 1500
B. C., we find a new language (Sanscrit) introduced
through the Vedas (Sacred Books) into India. The
civil institutions of Menu did not appear for two hundred
and twenty years after.

Father Marco, a Roman missionary, translated from
the Ramayan, through the Sanscrit into his native tongue,
to which he added a short mythological and historical
dictionary, in which he names Jirut a town and province
in which the priests from Egypt first settled in India ;
and Mr. Schmit gained a prize at the Academy of Inscriptions on an early Egyptian colony established in
India. That the Egyptians had strong, heavy, and well-
built sea-going vessels, is established from the writings
of both Herodotus and Pliny, and the paintings on the
early monuments show them to be fastened with nails
and pins, with spacious cabins well furnished, like those
of modern Egypt. If they had not been skilful navigators, they could not have defeated the fleets of Phœnicia,
or ventured to India. (Wilkinson, vol. iii., p. 189.) The
pine-apple models of glazed pottery found in the early

tombs were a large species, and are also found in the tombs contemporary with Joseph. We know that Necho, 3d Pharaoh of the 26th Dynasty, about 650 B. C., ascertained the peninsular form of Africa by doubling the Cape of Good Hope near 2,200 years before it was seen by Diaz, who was sent by John II. of Portugal. Emanuel, his successor, sent Vasco de Gama, in 1497, with orders to double it, and proceed to India.

The probability is, some Egyptian or Phœnician navigator, with an Egyptian colony, landed on the coast of South America about 1500 B. C. It is possible, and becomes probable, when we reflect that 2,000 years before Columbus was born, Solan, the great Athenian, stated that, while in Egypt, Sanches, a learned Egyptian priest, told him of *islands* in the Atlantic larger than Asia and Africa combined. He must have had reference to the continents of North and South America. The people were the same color, and the emblems (some of them at least) of religion bear too close a resemblance not to be copies. Sir Wm. Jones, page 55, claims that China, Japan, Mexico, and Peru, were all colonized from the same source.

EGYPTIAN.

The above emblem is found above the doors of the ancient Temples, along the banks of the Nile. Hieroglyphical scholars all agree that this winged globe and serpents was placed there by order of the ancient Egyptian priests, to represent the three attributes of God,—LOVE, POWER, and WISDOM.

SOUTH AMERICAN.

The above emblem, so closely resembling the Egyptian on page 52, was discovered by John L. Stephens, in 1839–40, during his travels among the ancient ruins of Central and South America. Next to its close resemblance to the Egyptian, is that we find it placed directly in the same place : to wit, over the Temple doors.

EGYPTIAN.

The above figure is also found carved in stone near the doors of the ancient Temples along the banks of the Nile.

SOUTH AMERICAN.

The above figure is also found carved in stone, and placed near the doors of the ancient Temples of Central and South America. All these emblems bear a close resemblance to each other, and must have had a common origin.

Mr. George E. Squires, who spent two years in exploring the Peruvian antiquities, remarks that the architectural remains, which are in many places stupendous, show proofs of skill and power equalling and sometimes surpassing those of Egypt. He was agreeably surprised on finding that numerous ancient edifices are still in use in nearly a perfect condition, having been converted into churches, convents, etc., and this is particularly true in the city of Cuzco. There the corners of the old streets are still preserved, with the walls of many buildings, and where the latter have been demolished, the gates still remain. Assisted by foreign engineers, he was able to make a complete plan of that old capital of the Incas. In many places the native architects availed themselves of natural facilities, procuring enormous stones from ledges above the sites of their constructions.

Some have supposed that the Hebrew and Phœnician languages were imitations of the arrow-headed Zen, it being the language stamped on the bricks of Babylon.

But the Rev. Dr. Lamb, of Cambridge University, has shown that the Hebrew alphabet can be traced, letter by letter, to a primitive Egyptian Hieroglyphic. To Thoth, Mercury, or the first Hemas, the Egyptians ascribe the invention of letters. He appears to be the type of the antediluvian revelation to man. He belongs to the fabulistic, shadowy, antediluvian period known in Egypt as the reign of the gods. The rule of the gods here mentioned has relation to priestly rule, or God ruling through the priests. The Egyptians did not believe that any Egyptian God ever lived on earth; the story of Osiris, ruler of the dead, is purely allegorical. (See Wilkinson's Thebes, p. 254, extract from Plato.)

Plutarch and Plato both affirm that the writing invented by the 1st Thoth, whom we call the antediluvian Hemas, differed from that invented, or re-discovered by

Thoth the 2d, which has come down to our day under the name of Hieroglyphics on the Nilotic Monuments of Egypt. Sanchoniathon Miso, who may be Mizraim, was the ancestor of *Jaautus*, the Egyptian Thoth Hemas, who invented the writing of the first letters. So Phœnician and Egyptian annals agree in attributing the invention of letters to the same personage.

How or in what manner the writing of the First Thoth differed from the Second, we have been unable to define. The Second Egyptian Thoth, without doubt, introduced the Hieroglyphical writing. And what more can we say in praise of Egyptian learning than to add that Plato, Tacitus, Pliny, Plutarch, Diodorus, and Champollion, all award to Egypt the honor also of inventing alphabetic writing. Prof. Rawlinson, in his laborious researches in the ruined cities of the Euphrates, thinks he has discovered remains of an ancient Turian Empire, which flourished and fell long before Nineveh, the first of which was established 2234 B. C., by a Hamatic prince of Elam. The second, 1976 B. C., by another Hamatic tribe from Susiana, which lasted until 1518 B. C. He remarks, they all bore Hamatic indications resembling Egypt. The Turian family embrace the Chinese and the greater portion of the Asiatic people, and in Europe the Fins and Laps, the Magyars and Turks, the Tartars, Mongols, Thibetians, Tamulians, and the Aboriginal Indian people, and all dialects of the Eastern Archipelago. Caldwell, Hodgson, Max Muller, and Bunsen so designate them.

Prof. Wilson, A. M., author of " Errors of Grammar and Nature of Language," page 316, remarks : " It is not many years since we were taught that the Chinese were a people without another with which to compare them and their language, in the whole wide world. But time and labor have made us wiser. We now know for a certainty that the roots of both the languages of that nation extend far back into the great Tartar Clans in the north and west, and into the Malay and Indian in South Asia. This language is the most infantile and uncultivated of any adopted by so large a portion of the human family, having two hundred and fourteen letters in its alphabet. In fact, within a few years the examination of the roots and structure of all languages has been brought to great perfection. Through this branch of learning it has been ascertained that what is called the Aryan Ind-European family of nations, have a common origin. The blonde Norwegian and the dark-eyed Spaniard, the Mercurial Kelt and the steady Anglo-Saxon, the Slavonic Russian and the Frenchman, the practical Anglo-American and dreamy Hindoo, the German and the Persian, the Greek and Roman, are proved to be all emigrants from one home, and to have spoken once a common tongue. By comparing the languages of the foregoing peoples with Sanscrit, which is the mother of twenty different living languages spoken in northern and southern India, the evidence becomes so clear that it is unassailable. Words conveying the simplest ideas of existence and action, nearest family relation, such as Father and Mother, Daughter and Son ; names of domestic animals, such as Pig, Goose, Duck, Sow, Boar, and Dog; words for the luminaries of the sky, words of feeling, such as Heart and Tears ;—these words show these tribes had made some progress in civilization before they separated. They had fastened animals to vehicles, built houses, worked in metals, constructed boats, and were acquainted with sewing and weaving. They most likely were engaged in pastoral life. The original home of the great Aryan family is hid in the mist of antiquity. Traditions of two of its branches designate the plateau of Asia, lying east of the Caspian, as their common home.

The Turanians, with their Nomadic language, were still older, and perhaps the first who figured as nations in Asia. The Aryan came after; then the Semitics. The Turanians include the wandering forest tribes, with little inclination to cultivate civilization. While there is no doubt that Ham accompanied his son Mizraim into Egypt ("And smote the first-born in Egypt; the chief of their strength in the tabernacles of Ham." Ps. lxxviii. 51), and carried with them the learning and civilization of the antediluvian world. This is rendered plausible by the language of Egypt being perfect on the first monuments, which implies that it was the one used by the antediluvians. One hundred Hieroglyphical characters being drawn from house furniture, which proves a civilized state when the Hieroglyphics were made, as all biblical commentators have agreed that Egypt was assigned to Mizraim, son of Ham, for a domain and for an inheritance, which is fully sustained by Egyptian history, wherein it is called the land of Khem.

Thus in the earliest period of Hieroglyphic writing, the Egyptians preserved the name of Ham through the name of their country. Some have supposed that the father of the Egyptians was under a curse; but if they will read from the twentieth to the twenty-seventh verse, ninth chapter of Genesis, they will see that Noah's prophetic denunciation was not of Ham, nor of Cush, nor of Mizraim, nor of Phut. But cursed be Canaan, the fourth and youngest son of Ham. Now Canaan, in direct contravention of the will of God, took possession of Palestine, the land destined for the posterity of Abraham. Thus some 1500 years after this event the Canaanites were ejected from Palestine, slaughtered or subjugated by the hosts under Josua. It was through Canaan's posterity that human sacrifice first originated ; their altars reeking with the blood of men. And it is not only in the Bible that Canaan is accursed, for Thebean monumental sculpture, carved about 1500 B. C., pronounced Kanana a barbarian country. But even in this moral wilderness we find exceptions, and meet with *oases*, for (Gen., fourteenth chapter and eighteenth verse) Melchizedeck, king of Salem, was a Priest of the most *High God;* a standing proof that the worst Gentile nation in Abraham's day had one man who followed the pure primeval creed, and both David and St. Paul agree in stating that Christ was constituted a priest forever after the order of Melchizedeck ; and the *Rev. Charles Burton, LL. D, F. L. S.,* in his lectures on the world before and after the flood (2d Volume, page 352, London edition), states : " We must, therefore, consider Melchizedeck, king of Salem, an earthly prince as much as the king of Sodom, and as truly a human personage as Abraham and Lot or any of the confederate kings mentioned in this narrative."

Neither Ham nor his three sons were cursed, for his name is associated with the richest, most fertile, and most ancient country of the earth, and stands in history as the founder of the most civilized and powerful nation of antiquity.

The first colonists who settled on the Lower Nile appear to have been already in a high state of civilization. It must be conceded that Mizraim and his descendants were the depositaries of all the magical and archæological secrets of the antediluvians.

As the earliest settlements were around the mouth of the Nile, it is probable that Ham and Mizraim came from some part of tropical Asia in ships, a few hundred years after the flood. As the climate of Europe, now the home of the white race, never was suited for the first dwelling-place and development of the human family, it is evident, if the first pair were created there, nature would have furnished natural clothing suitable for the maintenance of life without the aid of art. But man does not belong to the cold climates. His original birth-place has been in a region of perpetual summer, where the unprotected skin bears without suffering the slight fluctuations of temperature. He is, in fact, essentially a production of the tropics, and there has been a time when the human family, then all of one complexion (red), had not strayed beyond these geographical limits.

We take the following extract from Adelung's Mithridates. This great German linguist wrote many valuable works at Leipzig, during the latter part of the 16th century. He remarks, concerning the birth-place of man :

"We must fancy to ourselves this first tribe endowed with all human faculties, but not possessing all knowledge and experience, the subsequent acquisition of which is left to the natural operation of time and circumstances. As nature would not unnecessarily expose her first-born and unexperienced son to conflicts and dangers, the place of his early abode would be so selected, that all his wants could be easily satisfied, and everything essential to the pleasure of his existence, readily procured. He would be placed, in short, in a garden, or paradise.

"Such a country is found in central Asia, between the 30th and 50th degrees of north latitude, and the 90th and 110th of east longitude (from Ferro) ; a spot which, in respect to its height, can only be compared to the lofty plain of Quito, in South America. From this elevation, of which the great desert Cobi, or Shamo, is the vertical point, Asia sinks gradually toward all the four quarters. The great chains of mountains, running in various directions, arise from it, and contain the sources of the great rivers which traverse this division of the globe on all sides ;—the Selinga, the Ob, the Lena, the Irtisch, and the Jenisey, in the north ; the Jaik, the Jihon, the Jemba, on the west ; the Amur and the Hoang-ho (or Yellow River), toward the east ; the Indus, Ganges, and Burrampooter, on the south. If the globe was ever covered with water, this great table-land must first have become dry, and have appeared like an island in the watery expanse. The cold and barren desert of Cobi would not, indeed, have been a suitable abode for the first people ; but on its southern declivity we find Thibet, separated by high mountains from the rest of the world, and containing within its boundaries all varieties of air and climate. If the severest cold prevails on its snowy mountains and glaciers, a perpetual summer reigns in its valleys and well-watered plains. This is the native abode of rice, the vine, pulse, fruit, and all other vegetable productions from which man draws his nourishment. Here, too, all the animals are found wild which man has tamed for his use, and carried with him over the whole earth ;—the cow,* horse, ass, sheep, goat, camel, pig, dog, cat, and even the serviceable rein-deer, his only attendant and friend in the icy deserts of the frozen polar regions. Close to Thibet, and just on the declivity of the great central elevation, we find the charming region of Cashmire, where great elevation converts the southern heat into perpetual spring, and where nature has exerted all her powers to produce plants, animals, and man, in the highest perfection. No spot on the whole earth unites so many advantages ; in none could the human plant have succeeded so well without any care.† This spot, therefore, seems to unite all the characters of paradise, and to be the most appropriate situation in Asia for the birth-place of the human race."

Egypt forms the connecting link between Africa and the civilized world. It extends from the Mediterranean on the north, to Nubia on the south, distance about five hundred miles. The Syrian desert, without any definite line, forms the western, and the Red Sea the eastern boundary. The Nile, the great river of Africa, with its sweet-tasting water, originates from a lake, lately discovered by Mr. Baker, which he has named Albert Nyanza. This lake is two thousand seven hundred miles from the

---

* To determine the original stock of our domestic animals is one of the most difficult undertakings in zoology. I know no data on which the ox-kind can be referred to any wild species in Asia. Cuvier has concluded, from a minute osteological inquiry, that the wild ox (urus or bison of the ancients; aurochs of the Germans), formerly found throughout the greater part of temperate Europe, and still met with in the forests of Lithuania, of the Carpathian and Caucasian chains, is not, as most naturalists have supposed, the wild original of our cattle; but that the characters of the latter are found in certain fossil crania; whence he thinks it probable "that the primary race has been annihilated by civilization, like that of the camel and dromedary."—*Des Animaux fossiles*, v. iv. ; *Ruminans fossiles*, p. 51.

† Adelung; 11. Theil. *Einleitung*, pp. 3–9.

### William I.,

KING OF PRUSSIA.—Born October 15th, 1795; ascended the throne October 18th, 1861. Population of his kingdom, 24,039,545; religion, Protestant.

### John,

KING OF SAXONY.—Born December 12th, 1801; ascended the throne August 9th, 1854. Population of his kingdom, 2,423,601; religion, Protestant.

### Charles I.,

KING OF WURTEMBERG.—Born March 6th, 1823; ascended the throne June 26th, 1864. Population of his kingdom, 1,778,396; religion, Protestant.

### Abdul-Aziz-Khan,

EMPEROR OF TURKEY.—Born February 9th, 1830; ascended the throne June 25th, 1861. Population of his empire, 42,065,610; religion, Mahommedan.

### George I.,

KING OF GREECE.—Born December 24th, 1845; ascended the throne October 31st, 1863. Population of his kingdom, 1,348,522; religion, Greek Church.

### Frederic,

GRAND DUKE OF BADEN.—Born September 9th, 1826; ascended the throne April 24th, 1852. Population of his kingdom, 1,434,970; religion, Catholic.
This country contains the great watering-place of Europe.

mouth of the Nile, and two thousand four hundred and forty-eight feet above the level of the sea.

It is about as large as Scotland, and is fed by all the mountain streams of Central Africa. Thus the stream of the river which has been the wonder of all generations of men, has within the last four years been traced to its source. This river flows through Egypt, Nubia, Kordofan, and Abyssinia : a few miles below Cairo it separates and forms two branches, ninety miles from the sea. The eastern branch reaches the sea at Damietta, and the western at Rosetta. These two outlets are about eighty miles apart. Lower Egypt extends from the sea to Cairo. Middle Egypt extends from Cairo to Manfabout ; and Upper Egypt extends from the latter place to the Nubian border. Many great scholars in past ages entertained the opinion that civilization originated with the black race in Ethiopia, and descended the Nile. If this were true, it would be an argument against our evidence of the origin of color, and it would also be a death-blow to the future hopes of the black race and their friends. But it is not true. The negro, in his own native clime, has never yet embraced civilization : but that is no reason he never will. Persons we dislike, we immediately begin to find a reason in their race ; this is doubly so when we have done them a great and causeless wrong. Thus we dislike the people we have wronged, and a set of philosophers in the interest of slavery, went to work to prove that the man from Congo is not a man, because he is *black*, and has a thick *lip*. Then if he is a man, he is a poor, weak, degraded creature, who was always intended for a slave.

As it has been proved beyond controversy that the

oldest monuments in the valley of the Nile are found in Lower Egypt, about one hundred and twenty-five miles above the mouth of the river.   Here around Memphis, during the existence of the third, fourth, and fifth dynasties, were erected the mightiest pyramids, the most gigantic structures ever built by human hands.   It was at Memphis, during the latter part of the old monarchy, that Joseph dwelt, and ruled the land of Egypt under one of the wisest of its Pharaohs.   A little way beyond this oldest landmark of civilization begins the blessed region of Goshen, out of which Moses led the children of Israel to the Syrian desert.   It was here, according to tradition, that Mary rested with the infant Jesus.   And how many countless thousands have visited these wonders of the world before us, the youngest in time, and yet the predecessors of millions that will in other ages succeed. These pyramids were built for resting-places for the great dead.   Each king commenced the building of his pyramid as soon as he ascended his throne.   He only designed a small one to insure a complete tomb, even if he were to be but a few years upon the throne.   But in the advancing years of his reign he increased it in size by successive layers, till he thought he was near his end. If he died during its erection, then the external arena was alone completed, and the monument of death finally remained proportionate to the duration of the life of the king.   By these means, like the rings of a tree, posterity (all other conditions remaining) might be able to calculate the number of years he had reigned by the coating of the pyramid.   Every Pharaoh was the sun of Egypt, and over his name bore " Son of the Sun ;" and as the sun was Pharaoh, so each king was called Pharaoh.

Every monarch inherited his father's throne by lineal succession. In consequence, the incumbent was Pharaoh, son of Pharaoh. But a Pharaoh might, by his own barbarity or misrule, ostracise himself, so as to prevent his being buried even in his own tomb. This was a powerful stimulus to act justly and rule wisely and mercifully.

These monuments, one hundred and fifty in number, are strung along the banks of the Nile, up through Nubia to Meroe, a distance of fifteen hundred miles. The higher we ascend the Nile valley, the monuments become more modern, which caused Dr. Lepsius to remark, "that the most ancient epoch of art in Ethiopia was purely Egyptian, the oldest being only contemporary with the great Rameses, 1400 B. C., who, of all the Pharaohs, extended his domains not only further south but north."

Thus is established a new and interesting historic fact, that Egypt did not receive its civilization from the dark or Negro race, but whatever advance Ethiopia had made in civilization, was learned from the ancient *red race* of Egypt. (See Lepsius, pages 18 and 19.)

This is a heavy blow against the great antiquity of the Negro race, who first appear painted on the monuments of the eighteenth dynasty, 1500 B. C. Thus a historic period of twenty-five hundred years had passed before we have any evidence in Egypt of a *jet black* race. The inspired writer of the Book of Genesis, in his classification of humanity under the names of Shem, Ham, and Japheth, knew nothing of this race ; for the reason, that in his day none such were known. The Ethiopians were approaching black, very brown, and it is easy to conceive how many persons of their color, exiled or driven from Ethiopia beyond the border into Soodan, would die

while undergoing the change. But some must have
survived, and in a few thousand years Soodan was peo-
pled with a jet-black race with curly hair. When this
occurred we know not, but have no doubt it commenced
very early, perhaps at an ante-historic date ; as Dr. Lepsius, the late Prussian Nilotic explorer, has authoritatively
extended the history of the world back near two thousand years beyond Champollion. Others may still follow
with additional and other important developments. The
Hyksos, or Shepherd kings, first appeared and ruled
Egypt during the fourteenth, fifteenth, sixteenth, and seventeenth dynasties.

It was during their reign the Egyptian power was
driven into Ethiopia, and the ruling castes of both countries became somewhat mixed. The white race having
driven the rulers into Ethiopia, began to mix with the red
Egyptians left behind. It is about this period that yellow
women first appear painted on the monuments. Previously the native Egyptian women were always painted
red ; the Ethiopian women were represented by the same
color. But a great change was wrought, not only in
color, but in the general features of many of the Egyptian
rulers. After the seventeenth dynasty, the black and
white varieties had come from the cold and hot countries
into which their ancestors had immigrated, and witnessing
such a marked difference in complexions, they were as-
tonished at each other. The Egyptians, knowing they
inherited the primeval color, viewed the red race as par
excellence ; at this date they paint on the monuments
*red, white, yellow,* and *black* men. The mighty natural
cause which produced these changes in the complexion
of the human family were to the wise men of Egypt

unknown, and up to the present time has remained a
mystery. By the force of logic we have sprung the
mysterious lock ; perhaps the key did not fit all the parts,
but the bolt flew back, and you see the door stands open.

The Egyptians enslaved both the white and black
races. Joseph was sold by his brethren to some Arabian
merchants who took him into Egypt, where he was pur-
chased by the then reigning Pharaoh. Josephus and
Manetho both agree that from the immigration of Jacob
and his family into Egypt until the expulsion of the
Hyksos or Israelites, by Thuthmosis the 1st, was five
hundred and eleven years. The Bible says about four
hundred. The Israelites were in bondage there four
hundred years, while the black race, men, women, and
children, are painted and recorded as slaves on the monuments 1500 B. C. The black and white races were
equally despised by Egyptians, and they used them indis-
criminately as slaves. But things have changed. The
glory of the ancient civilization of the red race has de-
parted from Egypt.

In Greece and Rome it became remodelled to suit the
wants and fancies of the young and energetic white race,
whose early home was Europe ; and it is through this
channel the great blessings of Egyptian civilization are
now flowing. By steam and sail this race controls the
commerce of the seas. In fact, all the great arteries of
travel and trade, both on land and over the great deep,
are at its command. The steamboat, the ships, the rail-
cars, and even the caravans that cross all the great deserts,
are grasped by their energy and managed by their skill.
But let us not forget the mother race, nor despise the
teachings, when young, we received at her knee.

9

Are not, however, Egyptian studies, and the mythology, philosophy, and doctrines of that misrepresented race, interesting to the divine who attests the unity of the Godhead and the holy Trinity? Can the theologian derive no light from the pure primeval faith that glimmers from Egyptian hieroglyphics, to illustrate the immortality of the soul and a final resurrection? It is vain, in the present enlightened age, to shrink from the astounding evidences of a pure revealed religion, in existence among the Gentiles, in ages anterior to Abraham and Moses; or, with Tertullian, to anathematize these important inquiries; or, with him, to attribute the pure doctrines of remote antiquity to the forethought and machinations of the spirit of darkness. Will not the historian deign to notice the prior origin of every art and science in Egypt, a thousand years before the Pelasgians studded the isles and capes of the Archipelago with their forts and temples—long before Etruscan civilization had smiled under Italian skies? And shall not the ethnographer, versed in Egyptian lore, proclaim the fact, that the physiological and other distinctions of the human race began to develop soon after the distribution of mankind throughout the earth?

Philologists, astronomers, chemists, painters, architects, physicians, must return to Egypt, to learn the origin of language and writing—of the calendar and solar motion—of the art of cutting granite with a *copper* chisel and of giving elasticity to a *copper* sword—of making glass with the variegated hues of the rainbow—of moving single blocks of polished syenite, nine hundred tons in weight, for any distance, by land and water—of building *arches*, round and pointed, with masonic precision unsurpassed at the present day and antecedent, by two thousand years, to the "Cloaca Magna" of Rome—of sculpturing a *Doric column*, one thousand years before the Dorians are known in history—of *fresco* painting in imperishable colors—and of practical knowledge in anatomy.

Every craftsman can behold, in Egyptian monuments, the progress of his art four thousand years ago; and, whether it be a wheelwright building a chariot—a shoemaker drawing his twine—a leather-cutter using the selfsame form of knife of old, as is considered the best form now—a weaver throwing the same hand-shuttle—a whitesmith using that identical form of blowpipe but lately recognized to be the most efficient—the seal-engraver cutting, in hieroglyphics such names as SHOOPHO's, above four thousand three hundred years ago—or even the poulterer removing the *pip* from geese—all these, and many more astounding evidences of Egyptian priority, now require but a glance at the plates of Rosellini.

It is a sad, but too excruciatingly accurate conviction in the minds Champollion's disciples, that, had *all* the hieroglyphic legends of ancient Egypt been preserved to us, we should now possess a complete, unbroken, and authentic series of annals back to the remotest periods of conceivable postdiluvian time; when the ancestors of the Hebrews were mere nomads in Aramanea; when the Pelasgians were yet unborn; the Greeks, Persians, and perhaps the Phœnicians, had not been dreamed of; more than fifteen centuries before Troy fell, and much "more than thirteen hundred years before Solomon" founded the Temple of Jerusalem,—till we should approach the early hour, when mankind dwelt together on the plains of Shinar.

When we scan the mighty blessings that have come down the stream of time, we find it was in Egypt animals were first domesticated. Cattle, sheep, and wild animals, such as the Gazelle, the Ibex, or wild goat, and the Oryx, formed part of the stock of an Egyptian farm-yard. Here Lions were taught to perform the part of hounds, and of the Chita or hunting leopard of India. Cats were made retrievers in fowling excursions among the fens. Snakes were charmed, and monkeys were made to help gather fruit. Crocodiles, at the call of their name, would come out of the water and submit to have their ears bored like young ladies ; even Rarey and Van Amburgh, in training wild animals, fell short of the Egyptians. In fact, the treatment of sick animals was a subject for the Egyptian painter near five thousand years ago. The artificial hatching of eggs was also a very early, and almost universal practice. Cattle of every color, red, spotted, pibald, were in great abundance. Men only were allowed to pail the cows, and while they performed this domestic duty they always tied their legs. They caught fish with nets. Pork, the Egyptians never eat. And it was from them the Israelites learned to despise it. The reason the Egyptians refused to eat pork was on account of their firm belief in the doctrine of transmigration of souls. They believed that when a soul was rejected at the Judgment, as unfit to enter Paradise, it almost invariably returned to earth again in the form of a pig, therefore they refused to eat pork for fear they might be eating *one of their friends*. Thus the antipathy of the Jewish race to eating pork is explained.

And architecture and sculpture were brought to great perfection. The houses were mostly built of crude brick, stone being chiefly confined to sacred edifices. Egypt first invented the arch, one thousand years before it was known in Greece, and fifteen hundred years before it was used by the Romans. Bricks were baked in the sun ; and each one had to bear the official stamp. Making bricks was the employment of the Jews and other captives taken in war. You see frequently represented by paintings in the early tombs the various trades—glass-blowers, potters, gold-workers, weavers, dyers, carpenters, mat-makers, cabinet-makers, undertakers, leather-cutters, sculptors, painters, scribes, and weighers. The entire epitome of a man's life were the principal subjects for his tomb, which were kept ready for inscriptions, and, like coffins with us, on hand for sale. They had means of transporting immense blocks of granite hundreds of miles. The colossus of Rameses II. was brought one hundred and thirty-eight miles to Thebes ; its weight was eight hundred and eighty-seven tons. Whilst the hundred and twenty-seven columns of Parian marble, sixty feet high, that adorned the Ephesian temple of Diana, only weighed one hundred and fifty tons each. Herodotus speaks of one block that was moved a great distance, that weighed above five thousand tons. We know of no power, even since the discovery of steam, by which it could be done. The largest of the great pyramids, Shoophos, covers thirteen and a half acres ; and Pliny states that three hundred and sixty-six thousand men were constantly employed for twenty years in its construction, while ten years had previously been employed in quarrying the stone,—the weight of which is estimated at six million eight hundred and forty-eight thousand tons, making eighty-nine million and twenty-eight thousand cubic feet ; while its cost, at

two shillings for each cubic foot, amounts to above ten
million pounds sterling.   The passages, chambers, floors,
walls, and ceilings, are entirely built of the finest red
granite, while the paintings are beautiful, being preserved
as fresh as if done yesterday.   Its original height was
four hundred and eighty feet, being one hundred and ten
feet higher than St. Paul's in London, and forty-three feet
above St. Peter's at Rome.   This mightiest of all human
achievements was the production of the old monarchy,
which comprised the first thirteen dynasties.   And this
great pyramid was the work of Saophis or Shoophos, the
second Pharaoh of the fourth dynasty, 3426 B. C.

Semempses, fifth Pharaoh of the first dynasty, was
the inventor of fresco painting, and built a pyramid at the
Labyrinth about 3700 B. C., which is the oldest one existing in Egypt, although the Labyrinth itself was not
erected until the twelfth dynasty.   The middle monarchy
was commenced by Sesortesen, first of the fourteenth, and
continued until the end of the seventeenth dynasty.

This Pharaoh founded the great city of Thebes, which
extended thirty miles, having one hundred gates, and,
during the time of its splendor, could send two thousand
fighting men and two hundred chariots out of each gate.

We insert here the following letter from a correspond-
ent of the New York Herald of February 21, 1870.
The writer, under date of Cairo, December 27, 1869,
concerning the wonderful ruins at Thebes, remarks :

"Thebes is the great event of the Nile voyage.   Thither all eyes turn coming up the Nile.
The ruins are so vast and the glories of Thebes have so often been sung by poets and writers, that
all hearts yearn for them.   Thebes is described by Homer as

"'Pouring her heroes through a hundred gates—
Two hundred horsemen and two hundred cars
From each wide portal issuing to the wars.'

## Louis II.,

KING OF BAVARIA.—Born August 25th, 1845; ascended the throne March 10th, 1864. Population of his kingdom, 4,824,421; religion, Catholic.

## William III.,

KING OF THE NETHERLANDS, AND GRAND DUKE OF LUXEMBURG.—Born February 19th, 1817; ascended the throne March 17th, 1849. Population of his kingdom, 3,628,463; religion, Protestant.

## De Alcantara Pedro II.,

EMPEROR OF BRAZIL.—Born December 2d, 1825; ascended the throne July 20th, 1840, and was coronated July 18th, 1841. Population of his empire, 11,780,000; religion, Catholic. His father was the fourth emperor of Portugal, and when the French, in 1807, invaded that country, the royal family fled to Brazil, which was raised to the rank of a kingdom in 1815.

## B. Juarez,

PRESIDENT OF MEXICO.—Born 1807. A native Indian, of pure Aboriginal parentage, he became President in January, 1858. Population of the republic, 8,287,413; religion, Catholic.

## Ulysses S. Grant,

PRESIDENT OF THE UNITED STATES OF AMERICA.—Born April 27th, 1822. Through and by his military achievements, the greatest rebellion known in history has been crushed. His sword struck the shackles from the slaves, and saved his country from dismemberment. The people elected him as chief magistrate in 1868, and he was inaugurated March 4th, 1869. Through and by his administration the Fifteenth Amendment to the Constitution, giving the right of suffrage to the colored race, has been adopted, and during the first year of his term as President the national debt has been reduced about $100,000,000. Population of the United States about 40,000,000. All Religions are tolerated.

## Sir John Young,

GOV.-GENERAL OF BRITISH NORTH AMERICA. Area of square miles, 3,019,145; population over which he rules, 5,000,000.

"We were permitted to stay at Thebes two days, and I shall therefore give a description of the ruins as we saw them.  Contrary to the advice of good Sir Gardiner, we saw Luxor and Karnak the first day, and the second we employed in visiting the tombs of the kings, Assasseer, Abdel Koorneh, the Palace of Koorneh Ramesium, the Colossi of Memnon and Medeenet Aboo.

"THE EAST BANK.—Luxor stands on the east side, within a few yards of the landing-place.  Though half filled up by Arab huts, a mosque, and the American Consul's house, the half unoccupied will command wonder and admiration.  This temple was one of the greatest and most important in Thebes, yet in "Guides" it is spoken of disparagingly.  Sir Gardiner goes into a few details about it, but not as much as it merits, because of the bad effect the miserable mud huts within has upon it, and because they occupy the finest and best portion of it.  I think if it were cleared to the floor, that such a view as its seventy-two columned portico and its grand hall would present, could not be rivalled by anything Egyptian.  From the front pylon, which is that fronting Karnak northward, to the rear portico, the entire length of this grand temple is six hundred and thirty-eight feet.  Its entire breadth is not known, for the close mass of Arab huts within the courts effectually prevents measurement ; but by going in on all-fours into these Arab huts, you will be startled at the profusion of capitals which peep out from underneath, denoting the columns that support them.  That any villain of an Arab beggar should have dared to build his hut near the magnificent Luxor will be a matter of wonderment.  The thought is apt to strike one, that should Ismail Khedive scourge every one of those people away, after the manner of Him who drove out those who polluted the temple at Jerusalem, he would be doing a very great service to art, for without the least doubt much would be found below to enrich a museum.

'This temple, placed on higher ground than any others, must have appeared a fit rival to Karnak ; for from its stupendous pillars, its obelisks and its pylon may be seen rising magnificently and proudly above the mass of rubbish which cumbers it.  Before the front pylon stands a solitary obelisk of red granite, the mate of that which stands in the Place de la Concorde, Paris.  To the right and left are four colossi, defaced, scarred, mutilated, and buried to the rim of their crowns.  Entering the pylon you should come to a larger area, with covered cloisters on each side ; but this is all filled up with adobe huts and rubbish to the depth of forty feet.  Proceeding forward through a small lane past the mosque, you enter the Grand Assembly Hall, fourteen columns of which alone stand, but these are of the largest class, being eleven feet in diameter.  Further it is impossible to go from the front, so that steps must be retraced, and an entrance effected to the sanctuary and adyta from the rear.  In a lateral hall, near the sanctuary, two Corinthian pillars of an old Greek church stand.  Side by side with the gigantic columns of the Luxor temple, these columns of the Greeks appear puny and insignificant, and it is to the credit of Egyptian art to be placed in such juxtaposition to its Greek rival.

"From Luxor we hastened to Karnak, situated a mile and a half north of the former, along what was once an avenue of ram-headed sphynxes.  While on this road, give rein to fancy.  Imagine yourself one among thousands proceeding in stately procession to the Temple of Karnak, countless flags and standards streaming in the breeze, the types of Egyptian divinities held aloft by strong, armed men ; gayly-painted inscriptions, fantastically designed, wreathed around or flowing from them ; Pharaoh's ensigns before each division of the procession ; wild music of harp, timbrel, sackbut, and psaltery ; double and single flutes, rising in melodious symphony, clear and loud in the lucent air of Thebes ; while the king—even Pharaoh—is in his own chariot ; mayhap, Rameses the Great, returning from his conquest of the world, grander and loftier than any of his subjects; the gay chargers such as were only reared for a Pharaoh's foeman as proudly as if they knew they were to grace a Pharaoh's triumph ; and the chariot is of gold and silver, sparkling with precious stones, with its war furniture, its bow and quiver, ornamented to the height of Egyptian skill ; and Pharaoh's nobles, in their robes of state, wend after him ; and the priests, in snowy linen, bordered with crimson, are before him, lifting on high their voices in the song of victory, and behind all come the cavalry, on their chargers from Ethiopia and Libya, with their burnished arms of bronze and brass ; and the infantry, with battle-axe and bow, spear and sword, with standards waving, trumpets sounding ; and the people of Thebes, the mercenaries and slaves, by thousands follow on foot to see the scenes of that day, while over all shines the warm sun of Thebes. This takes place in the year 2670 of the creation, and the year 1330 before Christ.  Pass over seven hundred years.  The same sun shines over Thebes, its temples and its palaces cover the plain, the same river flows hard by the temples of Karnak and Luxor, the same azure heaven vaults the Theban plain, which is as green and fertile as ever ; but a day of the year 519 b. c. has come, and the doom of Thebes immortalized is sealed, for the madman Cambyses, with his army, is marching from Luxor to Karnak.

" For deities represented by animals—for Osiris, the founder of the Egyptian monarchy, represented by the bull Apis—the goddesses Isis, Athor, and Phthah, represented by hawks and cats— Cambyses, the Persian, has no respect.   Neither knows he Aimin-Re, who has made Karnak temple his abode ; he knows not ambitious Mandu, with the inevitable hawk's head ; therefore he issues the order for the demolition of the statues, for the defacement of the sculpture, for the destruction of the matchless temple.   And thus the city of Thebes, the hecatompylean city, becomes a waste.   After the invasion of Cambyses, the Egyptians made an effort, and succeeded for a while, in re-establishing their independence, and Thebes once more took her former greatness.   Once more travellers came from afar to feast their eyes upon the Theban wonders—the fathers of history, Diodorus Siculus, Strabo, and others ; but the fiat has gone forth and there is none to stay it—a worse than Cambyses came, whose name was Lathyrus.   What remained after Lathyrus, travellers see now-a-days at Thebes.

" The matchless avenue of sphynxes, which lined the whole distance from Luxor to Karnak three thousand five hundred years ago, may be traced for about half the distance.   You may say about the great blocks which lie crumbling on each side of you, these were sphynxes once, but few of them retain that figure and form now.   About half-way to Karnak you will come to a square hollow, in which there are about sixty statues of Phthah of black granite, many of which are still upright.   This hollow was the terminus of a temple.   Proceeding a short distance further on, you see a solitary pylon, and the foundations of a temple may be traced.   Pass over the other pylonæ and march obliquely to the left, so that you may arrive at the front of the great Temple of Karnak.   Ah ! that temple !   So many eminent writers have described it, so many travellers have wailed in sympathy over its fallen state, so many poets have sung over it, what shall a young American say of Karnak ?   Take your Sir Gardiner in hand, or your Mr. Lane, or your Champollion, and each of them will guide you over the ruins.   But, in spite of this learned coterie, you will fain linger before the temple pylon, look up the stately height of the propylæ, at the wide embrasures in its front, at the colossi sculptured thereon, at the ruinous masses of stone looking but freshly fallen, to the vista of columns, and halls, and obelisks, sanctuaries, and walls, as you stand minion-like in the portal.   Great is the Parthenon, enthroned upon the Athenian Acropolis ; great is the Coliseum at Rome with its sad history ; great are the Sagantine ruins and Gothic

Avilla, but greater, grander, statelier by far, stands Karnak temple. You pass under the pylon and you come to a spacious area, which measures two hundred and seventy-five feet by three hundred and twenty-nine feet; another pylon and a vestibulum terminates this, which is about fifty feet in depth, and you are in the famous hall of Karnak with its one hundred and forty pillars, awe-struck by their gigantic size and its aspect. This hall measures one hundred and seventy by three hundred and twenty-nine feet. You could put the whole of Trinity church within it, and have a clean passage round about it afterward, between the walls of the hall. Another hall succeeds this with an obelisk stair standing, one of a pair which stood before the pylon of another hall beyond this, where there is a taller obelisk, and measuring eight feet square. This latter hall is surrounded by osiride pillars, all of which, however, are mutilated. Beyond this is the sanctuary of sanctuaries, constructed of exquisitely polished red granite, with a host of adyta and lateral aisles and passages surrounding it. Beyond this is another hall, and still another until you have arrived at the circuit wall, and have traversed the length of eleven hundred and eighty feet. A temple eleven hundred and eighty feet long by three hundred and twenty-nine feet wide! What is St. Peter's at Rome to this?

"But you will not be induced to rush so hurriedly through the temple as all this. The great hall of Karnak will hold you spell-bound. You will wonder at its length, at its breadth, at its height, at the finite and colossal tracery of chisel over it, at its stupendous columns, rising sixty-two feet from the floor and eleven feet in diameter; at the patches of brilliant and exquisite coloring you will see here and there, and you will want to imagine all this when it was new. Then the obelisks, with their tops spiring into the clear air and pointing to the all-serene heaven of Thebes, will demand your attention, and the massive osirides, thirty feet in height, each composed of a single block; the beautiful ornature of the sanctuary and its surroundings; the lintel stones, forty feet in length; each and all these are subjects of wonder. Yet these are but a tithe of what is to be found at Karnak. Mount the circuit walls, the lofty pylon facing the Nile, or the still loftier propylæ, or the summit of a gigantic column in the hall. Look around, below, above, and admiration succeeds to admiration, wonder to wonder. As for the sculptures on the walls, they are too varied for detail. Could one but read them, much of the history of Egypt might be read, both sacred and profane. Going into this temple to look at the sculptures, is just like going to the Louvre at Paris. Napoleonic and war history of France may be read in the latter; why not Egyptian history in the former? The Louises and the Napoleons are seen at the front of Balbec pictures on the walls of the Louvre; the great Rameses or some other Pharaoh may be seen on the temples of Prosopolis Magna, or modern Karnak.

"The second day we crossed the river to visit the colossi of Memnon, and the tombs and temples of the western bank. The modern name of the king's tombs is Bab el Molook, signifying the 'gates of the kings.' The gate of the kings! What a fit signification! For none but kings entered therein, and it opened to death!

"The Libyan range is at Thebes, just two miles from the Nile, at a point opposite Koorneh. At this point a ravine opens in the range of hills to the width of about two hundred feet. When you enter it you are in the most desolate, dreary, forbidding, barren, stony region in the world. Not a blade of grass, no, not one, nor shrub, nor any green thing is visible; it is brown limestone rising in strata from the bottom of the ravine to the summit of the hill on either side, while the base is covered with debris, great rocks crumbling or crumbled, over which the sun pours its fiercest every day throughout the year. You follow this ravine, winding and deviating from point

to point, for a mile and a half, until you are halted by a cross hill, which bars all further proce-
dure. Here are the tombs of the kings, so far opened to the number of twenty-one, each one of
which is a palace cut and chiselled out of the solid rock, stuccoed and painted all over. There
are forty-seven of them in this valley, but twenty-six of them remain undiscovered, where it may
be supposed kings still lie, 'every one in his own house.' Keen-sighted, knowing travellers have
been here, Belzoni among the keenest, yet there are twenty-six still undiscovered, which is, perhaps, all the best for the great dead who still lie there, but nevertheless a loss to Art. If one had
only the money, they could be discovered doubtless, but moneyed travellers are not often found
who could spare time and money to proceed to work. Some day, I hope, we shall have a national
museum in New York, and some enterprising man, with the proper spirit and ambition, will fill
an Egyptian room with the riches of these undiscovered tombs.

"THE TOMBS.—Sir Gardiner Wilkinson, for the better description of them, has numbered
them in red paint, respectively from one to twenty-one. Number seventeen was discovered by
Belzoni, and is the most superb of all for the spaciousness of the halls within and the exquisite
paintings which adorn its walls. These paintings generally treat of religious subjects, of the death
of kings, and the transmigration of souls through various subsequent stages. One particular king,
Settici I., father of Rameses the Great, is recognized in all these sets of paintings. He is represented offering sacrifices to Osiris and Isis, as being judged by Osiris the judge of the dead, while
the goddess of truth and justice stands by. In another place he is seen accepted by Osiris, who
holds out his sceptre toward him, as Ahasuerus is said to have done to Esther, his queen. One
hall to the right, at the furthest end, is not quite completed. You may trace a pencilling of red,
with another of black over it, as if a master artist had superintended the work. The outlines are
bold and masterly, and they have not all that stiffness which the skeleton drawing of Sir Gardiner
would lead one to believe, and the paintings present Egyptian dress most vividly. You could
almost tell of what those rich raiments in which the figures are painted were made of. The tomb
penetrates three hundred and twenty feet into the rock, and over wall and ceiling of passage and
hall is placed the stucco, which has retained the paintings for over three thousand years.

"Tomb number eleven, called the Harper's tomb, from the figure of a harper, which is seen
at the extreme chamber to the right of the passage. This also is painted with interesting subjects.
The monarch for whom this tomb was constructed is Rameses III. It is four hundred and five
feet in length, and arranged in halls like number seventeen, but does not descend so abruptly into
the ground.

"Tomb number six is highly interesting, though not so well preserved as the two above mentioned ; still the subjects, which are of a widely different character, are even fresher, but not painted
with the taste and skill of the former. On the right of the entrance passage is a section of the
wall devoted to the illustration of generation and gestation, which prove the ancient Egyptians to
have been far behind the moderns in human anatomy. On the wall behind the sarcophagus the
youthful Adonis is depicted seated on a globe, and according to Sir Gardiner, who is learned in
Egyptology, it is thought to refer to the theory that dissolution is followed by reproduction
into life.

"Tomb number two was open during the time of the Greeks in Egypt, and numerous are the
inscriptions on the walls of eminent Greek and Roman visitors. Of all which are open, this tomb
is the most elegant. It descends on an incline of five feet in fifty ; you may ride two horses
abreast to the furthest end of the tomb safely at a hand gallop. A most beautiful sarcophagus of

red granite is found at the end of the tomb, a little frayed on one side by the rapacious hands of souvenir gatherers. This tomb is the great resort for those who wish to lunch after visiting the four best specimens of kings' sepulchres, as these are all that the unlearned in antiquity care to visit.

" 'By the life of Pharaoh,' I repeat, those ancient Egyptians were giants. Continual visits during a Nile voyage into their tombs and temples stamps a clearer idea of them on the mind than all the books that could be read, and they inspire respect and respectful admiration for them, notwithstanding the terrible aspect of frowning colossi, or the dread look of Pharaoh while smiting his captives.

"CATACOMBS.—From these royal abodes of death—this Tophet of a valley—travellers generally hasten to visit the catacombs of Assaseef. Sir Gardiner praises one of them most enthusiastically, . because it was eight hundred and sixty-two feet long, when he wrote his book, and had many chambers and great halls; but since that time the Arab miners have destroyed the finest portions of it, so that it is actually not worth visiting; besides, the mephitic odor issuing out in strong, deathly currents would kill the keenest of interests. Neither are the tombs of Abdel Koorneh interesting. One feels inclined to laugh at Sir Gardiner for his zeal. The paintings alone at number thirty-five will repay a visit.

"The small temples of Dayr el Bahree and Dayr el Medeeneh are very interesting, and well worth the trouble of a visit to them, but I have no space to describe them, other portions of Thebes more important deserve attention.

"The Ramesium or Memnonium lies directly below the grottoes of Koorneh. Though in a most ruinous state, with but the portico and propylæ standing, the Ramesium is a favorite with all visitors. All admire the bell formed of lotus-flower capitals, as well as the columns of the portico, because they do not present that heaviness which the crowded state of others naturally had; and they are finer sculptured, besides being in better proportion to the size of the portico. From a distance the Ramesium looks as imposing as any in Egypt. One reason for this is that its ruins, its portico, its propylæ, are much higher than the red mounds of debris which always are found in the vicinity of Egyptian temples. The real grandeur and charms of the temple ruins of Egypt are obscured by these mounds, which, in very many instances, such as before Dendera and Abydos, rise higher than the ruins themselves. For a parallel case, imagine the national capitol at Washington surrounded by refuse heaps rising to a level with the summit of the dome; where would the grandeur and the beauty of it be? Do men light a candle and put it under a bushel? For the reason, then, that the Ramesium is more freed from obstructing dust hills and mud huts, and what is left of it is seen to good advantage from afar, it is that travellers as soon as they descry its ruins yearn to view them closer.

"This temple palace was six hundred feet in length from portico to circut wall, by one hundred and eighty feet in breadth, but the greater part of it is in too ruinous a state to enter into details.

"Before the portico lie the ruins of the largest statue in Egypt, of eight hundred and eighty-seven tons in weight, so says Sir Gardiner. It is a monster statue of sienite granite polished as smooth as a mirror. The iconoclastic hands of the Arabs have been laid upon this also, for they have constructed millstones from the face, so that this hero of a statue was not even respected when low. Iron-hearted Cambyses smote it at the legs and levelled 'it from its pedestal to the dust, but pagan Arabs with chisel and hammer defaced it.

"THE COLOSSI.—From the Ramesium to the colossi of Memnon is but a step. Now you stand in the shadow of the famous colossus, and repeat to yourself the sweet tradition which fable has woven about it.    There are two colossi seated on thrones about fifteen paces apart, looking eastward, but there is only one vocal Memnon, which is the northernmost or the one nearest to the Ramesium.    The story goes that, every morning at sunrise, a sound issued from it similar to the breaking of a harp-string.    Strabo, whose curiosity must have prompted him to rise early to satisfy it, says that he heard a sound, but whether it proceeded from the statue or from some one in the crowd—for there were curious people in Thebes itself—he was not certain.    But there were not wanting those who affirmed stoutly that the sound emanated from Memnon when the sun touched its lips.    Every morning Memnon sung, 'Oh, sweet story ; oh, romantic fable.'    It prompts you to look kindly at Memnon, wishful that it were true.    What a charm is there in a well-devised story !    Sir Walter Scott has restored knight errantry from the obloquy into which the satiric pen of Cervantes had cast it.    Washington Irving has made all English readers love the simple 'Rip Van Winkle,' but here fable, with a simple story of two or three words, makes you reverence a stone, while its mate, much better preserved, is disregarded.    The lips, eyes, and the points of Memnon's feet have been destroyed.    Its entire body was also broken in pieces by that mad Cambyses who has been the bane of Egypt, but Severus restored it with huge blocks of sandstone chiselled in the form of the deity we see to-day.

"To climb to the lap of Memnon is a labor even to active young men ; but what young student would not do it, so that he could say he had sat in great Memnon's lap !    When a traveller visits Versailles or the Trianon, he must sit in the chair of Napoleon or Josephine.    When he visits the royal palace at Madrid, he must needs throw himself into the chair of Philip IV. and test the luxury of Isabella's couch.    How much greater is the honor of having sat in the lap of Memnon, the dutiful son of the morning !"

All that now remains of this great empire are the wonderful ruins above described, and a mixed and scanty population consisting of twenty thousand Turks, who occupy all the prominent positions ; one hundred and fifty thousand Copts, who claim to be the descendants of St. Mark ; two million Asiatics ; two hundred thousand Bedouins, the descendants of Ishmael ; and a few French and Jews, who are the money changers of the country.

But to return to its former history.    The new monarchy commenced with Amos of the eighteenth dynasty ; and it was under Tuthmosis III., sixth Pharaoh of this dynasty, that the Hyksos were driven from the frontiers, and the Israelites sorely oppressed.    The Hyksos were

### Prof. Ed. W. Blyden,

OF LIBERIA COLLEGE, MONROVIA, AFRICA.—This eminent man is of pure African blood, and was born August 3d, 1832, in St. Thomas, one of the Danish West India islands. He came to New York in 1850 with Mrs. Knox, wife of Rev. John P. Knox, where he accepted the offer of the New York Colonization Society to furnish a passage to Liberia. Arriving there, he entered the Alexander High School. In 1858 he had sole charge of that institute, when in 1869 he was elected Professor of Languages in the Liberia College, delivering the opening Inaugural Address, and now, 1870, speaks and writes 18 different dialects.

### Africa.

NEGRO MAN, Native of the great Desert of Sahara.—From time immemorial, this part of Africa has been the home of the woolly-haired race. It was here, Mongo Park and Capt. Carpenter lost their lives. Their king has such a vast number of wives, that he boasts that, linked hand in hand, they would reach from one end of his kingdom to the other.

### Africa.

ABBAS GREGORIUS.—A native of Abyssinia, and a descendant of the ancient Ethiopian stock. He was a great Linguist, especially in Ethiopian dialects, and it was by him the great German scholar Ludolph was instructed in the languages and history of Africa.

### Africa.

MALE NATIVE OF HOWSSA, Interior of Africa.—Jackson, Dedham, and Clapperton, celebrated travellers in that part of the country, speak highly of the people as being acute and industrious,

### Africa.

NATIVE OF SOODAN, or LAND OF THE BLACKS. Woolly-haired type of Central Africa.—They roam over a vast region of country, with limits undefined.

### Toussaint L'Ouverture.

Born in St. Domingo of African slave parents, May 20th, 1743, he headed the revolt in that island in 1791, and was 50 years old before he commenced military life. By courage and generalship in the field in many hard-fought battles he, at the head of the black race, became master of the island, subduing the Spaniards, French, English, and Mulatto pop. In 1801, Napoleon sent a fleet and 35,000 troops under command of Gen. Le Clerc to reduce the island again to slavery under French rule. By the treachery of the French officers he was captured July 5th, 1802, and sent a prisoner to France, where, in a dungeon cell in Castle Joux in the Jura mountains, by order of Napoleon, he was starved to death by the keeper. August 27th, 1803.

white. They conquered, ruled, and almost destroyed Egypt during the fourteenth, fifteenth, sixteenth, and seventeenth dynasties of the second monarchy, and are known in Egyptian history as the "Shepherd Kings." The last monarchy ended with Nectanebus, 339 B. C.

We have previously shown that not only Hieroglyphical, but alphabetical writing has been traced to the red race of Egypt. So also the domestication of animals, invention of the arch, and manufacture of brick. We have shown that nearly all the mechanical trades were represented on the earliest monuments. Are there yet more blessings that the mother of civilization conferred upon the human race? Yes; the discovery of astronomy. The first recorded observatory must have been on the tomb of Semempses, the fifth Pharaoh of the first dynasty of the old monarchy, about 3700 years B. C. It had in it twenty thousand volumes, many of them the writings of Thoth Hermes. It contained a golden circle of two hundred feet in diameter; some have contended that the temple of Belus in Babylon contained the oldest table. But the matter is set at rest by Diodorus, i. 28. He says, "It is indeed supposed that the Chaldeans of Babylon, being an Egyptian colony, arrived at their celebrity in astronomy in consequence of what they derived from the priests of Egypt. The Babylonish method of dividing the year was the same as the Egyptian, and can be traced back to the Nile. Bailly maintains that astronomy was cultivated in Persia 3209, in India 2952, in Chaldea 2800 B. C. There is evidence the Hindoos determined the mean motions of *Saturn* and *Jupiter* 2952 B. C. It is true, when Alexander took Babylon, 330 B. C., Calisthenes found the Chaldean astronomers had made observations extending back nineteen hundred and three years. But we have shown that it existed in Egypt 3700 years B. C., or about seven hundred and fifty years before any record of it is found in either Persia, Chaldea, or India. Naerasch, an Egyptian priest, is believed to be the discoverer, as he was the first to represent the Zodiac by twelve signs. (See Book of Astrology by Raphael, page 21, London, 1828.) In fact, no other people, except the Egyptians, would be likely to confer a sign on water, such as Aquarius ; and it is reasonable to suppose that it would be made to accord with the flood, or fall of the Nile. And then, the other names, Ram, Bull, Twins, Crab, Lion, Virgin, Balance, Scorpion, Archer, Goat, Fishes, are all more applicable to Egypt than any other country. The Zodiac is a great circle, extending quite round the heavens, nearly sixteen degrees broad, so as to take in the different orbits of the planets, as well as the earth's satellite, the moon. In the middle of this circle is the ecliptic, or the path of the sun. 2d. All that region of the heavens which is on the *north* side of the zodiac, containing twenty-one constellations. And 3d. The whole region on the *south* side, which contains fifteen -constellations. That the Chinese, the Chaldeans, and Hindoos, became almost perfect in astronomy, is true ; but, like the boy the giant lifted on his shoulders, they saw further and no thanks. Like Archimedes and Apollonius, who followed Euclid, they only perfected what had been founded. Yes, the Egyptians discovered astronomy, and understood perfectly the geography of the heavens. They understood the cycle of the sun and moon ; the former is the twenty-eight years before the days of the week return to the same days of

### Africa.

NATIVE OF MOZAMBIQUE, EAST AFRICA.—This tribe was the first one called KAFIRS by Europeans, who learned the epithet from Mohammedan navigators of the Indian Ocean. Capt. Owen remarks, the farther from the coast, the more the natives improve in appearance. Ivory is the chief export of their country. About 250,000 pounds are sent annually to India.

### Africa.

JAN TZATZOE, Kafir of Amakosa tribe, Eastern Africa, and a Military man of some note among his own people.— Some of the Kafir tribe have the prominent nose of the Europeans and high cheekbones of the Hottentots. They are generally tall and strong, and number in all ab. 350,000 souls.

### Africa.

NATIVE OF ANGOLA.—The Angola's, Kongo's, and Loango's, which resemble each other, are now united under the sovereignty of the Manikongo, extending over the region on the western coast to a distance of 300 leagues in length by the sea side, and 200 in breadth, and contains a great portion of the high mountain land of Southwestern Africa.

### Africa.

FEMALE NATIVE OF ANGOLA, WEST AFRICA.—All the specimens of wild animals known in Africa, are found here. This country has always been notorious as the great centre of the slave market. Through the Portuguese slave trade about 35,000 slaves are annually carried from this country to the different slave marts of the world.

### Africa.

KOSAU KAFIR, a man of Eastern Africa. Portrait taken by Mr. Daniels.—There are several different tribes of the Kafir race, generally a Nomadic people, having considerable herds of cattle, and invariably practice the Jewish right of Circomcision—black Jews. Milk is their chief support. This is an inferior type of the Kafir race.

### Stephen A. Benson,

II. President of the Republic of Liberia.—Born of free, pure African parentage in Cambridge, Dorchester Co., Md., March 1816, he emigrated with his parents to Liberia in 1822. When there but a few months, he was captured by the savages in their wars on the colony, but afterward returned. He is a man of liberal education, which he acquired in Liberia. Roberts, the 1st president, was elected Oct. 5th, 1847; Benson was the 2d; Daniel B. Warren the 3d; James S. Payar the 4th, and Edward J. Roye now, 1870, the 5th. Roberts and Payar were about one-half white. Roye is about one-eight white, while Benson and Warren were both pure-blooded Africans. Population of Liberia, civilized ab. 18,000; of Africa, about 150,000,000. All Religions are tolerated in Liberia.

the month; the moon in nineteen lunar years and seven intercalary or nineteen solar years. They divided the year first into twelve lunar months, of twenty-eight days; they then substituted solar for lunar months of thirty days, or three hundred and sixty days in the year; and subsequently they added five complementary days to the twelve solar months, making the civil year three hundred and sixty-five days: and this was the only year known to Herodotus and Plato. They afterward discovered that the sidereal, or the complete revolution of the earth round the sun, takes six hours, nine minutes, and nine seconds, and a sixth of a second longer than the three hundred and sixty-five days. Thus making their system perfect.

The compass is supposed to have been discovered in China. Marco Polo introduced it 1290 B. C., twelve years before Gioca of Arnolfi, its supposed inventor.

The Egyptians discovered Chemistry, and were the first to have regular physicians. In this art they arrived at great perfection, as there were eye doctors, and others for the ear. Midwifery was entirely under the direction of women. This doctoring of the different parts of the human body led to the science of Anatomy, the discovery of which has been, we have no doubt, wrongly attributed to Erasistratus and Herophilus, as Hermes and Athothes, both Egyptian Pharaohs, wrote works on anatomy.

While men in other regions were tyrannizing over the weaker sex, we have incontrovertible evidence that above 3700 years B. C. there was no *Salic* law in Egypt, but females were admitted to a full participation of all legitimate privileges with man. And Herodotus asserts that the Egyptians were not allowed to take more than one wife, and she was buried in the same tomb with her

husband.   The females in Egypt were honored, civilized, and educated.   If the king was without male
issue, daughters were queens by inheritance.   In fact,
they were as free as our American ladies ; and this
is an honored distinction between the social system
of ancient Egypt and the Jews, where the female was
never placed on an equal social position with the male,
and it was the same in all other oriental nations, and this
distinction is a standing proof of their high civilization.
They guarded strictly the political rights of their women,
as well as their social virtues.   In religion they worshipped the Creator by deifying his most marked, virtuous, and powerful attributes, as developed through creation.   They approached Amun, who was lord of all the
gods of Egyptian mythology, and the same as the Greeks
and Romans called Jove.   They approached him through
their various chosen gods—as the Christian, during the
early ages, looked up to the Saviour through the Cross.
No person in his rational mind can believe that people
so enlightened as the Egyptians worshipped absolutely
the creatures.   No, never.   They believed that Knum,
the creative power, moulded the mortal part of Osiris,
the father of men, out of a lump of clay ; the clay is
placed in the potter's wheel, which he turns with his foot,
while he fashions it with his hands.*   This figure is of
great antiquity, and was taken from the Mystic Chamber
of the Temple of Philæ, first Cataract.   Amur Neph
represents the creative power, that is, the Spirit of God,
the Breath of life.   Joshua, liv. 8 : " But now, O Lord,
thou art our potter, and we are all the work of Thy hand."
This bears a strong resemblance to a common tradition.

* See engraving, next page.

KNUM, THE CREATIVE POWER, MOULDING THE MORTAL PART OF OSIRIS, THE FATHER OF MEN.

TRANSLATION.

" 'Knum, the Creator, on his wheel moulds the divine members of Osiris (the type of man) in the shining house of life'—that is, in the solar disc."

"The god AMUN-KNEPH, turning a potter's wheel, moulding the mortal part of Osiris, the Father of men, out of a lump of clay. The clay is placed on the potter's wheel, which he turns with his foot, while he fashions it with his hands. It is a subject from the mystic chamber of the Temple of Philæ—1st Cataract.

"AMUN-KNEPH, or Neph, Kneph, Chnouphis, Noub—represents the 'creative power of Amun'—that is, 'the *spirit* of God'—the *breath* of *life* poured into our nostrils."

This figure, with the illustrations on the following page, is a standing proof that the ancient Egyptians, long before Abraham's day, worshipped the true God.

On the TEMPLE of SAIS, in Thebes, was inscribed, concerning the true God, this eternal truth :

" *All that hath been, I am ; is, and shall be ; and my covering hath no one yet removed: my offspring is the sun.*"

11

"He moulds man; in Hebrew, Adam, the first man, meaning both *man* and *red earth*, or clay. Now consult Isaiah, lxiv. 8 : 'But now, O Lord, thou art our Father : We are the *clay* (in Hebrew Adme, red earth), and thou our *potter ;* and we are all the work of *thy hand.*'"

May

thy soul

attain (come)

to

Khnum (one of the forms of Amon, the creator)

the creator (the idea denoted by a man building the walls of a city)

of all

Mankind (literally *men* and *women*).

'"May thy soul attain to Khnum, the Creator of all mankind."

"This alone is a proof of the primitive Egyptian creed of one God, the Creator (whose divine attributes were classed in triads), of man's possession of a soul, and of its immortality ; of a resurrection, and of the hope of such.

"Let it stand, for the present, as an insight into the pristine purity of Egyptian belief, in ages prior to Abraham's visit ; and let the constant expression of 'beloved of a god,' 'loving the gods,' like the Hebrew, 'dilectus a Domine suo, Samuel' (in the Vulgate), 'beloved of his Lord, Samuel,' attest the primeval piety of the Nilotic family over all contemporary nations, whom we are pleased to condemn as Pagans.

Abraham went into Egypt, and brought out with him an Egyptian woman whom he called Hagar. This woman bore him a son, and they called his name Ishmael; after this his other or first wife Sarah bore him a son also, and they called his name Isaac. Now it is said that God gave Abraham the covenant of circumcision, through which he was to preserve in all coming ages a separate and distinct people. Almost every person believes this sacred Jewish rite originated with Abraham. But it is not so. The Egyptians had practised circumcision from time immemorial, thousands of years before the Jewish race existed, or Abraham was born. For proof of this, see Bishop Russell, Wilkinson, Gliddon, Sharpe, Champollion, Rossellini, Lepsius, and a host of others. And Acosta, and Lopez de Gomara (among the earliest writers of aboriginal history), and so do Adair and Elias Boudinot, assert that the Indians of North America did the same. (Mariano Edward Rivero, Peruvian Antiquities, p. 9.)

Then we come to one of the cardinal doctrines of the Christian church : I mean the Resurrection from the dead and general judgment after death. Paul bases the whole doctrine of the Christian church on the Resurrection of Christ from the dead : " If the dead rise not, ye are yet in your sins, and our preaching is vain, and your faith is also vain."

The doctrine of the Resurrection was taught in Egypt twenty-five hundred years before the Saviour was born. On page 130 of " Wilkinson's Egypt," that highly gifted author remarks : " The Last Judgment is one of the principal subjects in the Egyptian tombs."

Last Final Judgment of the Dead, as taught by the Priests of Egypt 2500 years B. C.

JUDGING THE DEAD.—Description of the same, with names of actors in the scene, as painted in the early Egyptian tombs.

1. The forty-two Assessors—Judging after death and before burial.

"The relatives of the deceased announce to the judges, and to all the connections of the family, the time appointed for the ceremony, which includes the passage of the defunct over the lake or canal of the Nome to which he belonged. Two-and-forty judges are then collected, and arranged on a semicircular bench (only twenty-six of the Assessors can be seen on the engraving), which is situated on the bank of the canal; the boat is prepared, and the pilot, who is called by the Egyptians *Charon*, is ready to perform his office; whence it is said that Orpheus borrowed the mythological character of this personage. But before the coffin is put into the boat, the law permits any one who chooses to bring forward accusations against the dead person; and if it is proved that his life was criminal, the funeral honors are prohibited; while, on the other hand, if the charges are not substantiated, the accuser is subjected to a severe punishment. If there are no insinuations against the deceased, or if they have been satisfactorily repelled, the relations cease to give any further expression to their grief, and proceed to pronounce suitable encomiums on his good principles and humane actions; asserting, that he is about to pass a happy eternity with the pious in the region of Hades. The body is then deposited with becoming solemnity in the catacomb prepared for it."*

Judging the *secret actions* of the soul, good and bad, after the assessors had given the verdict.

2. HARPOCRATES.
3. OSIRIS, Judge of the Dead.
4. Four GENII of Armenti, standing on a lotus leaf.
5. HORUS introduces the deceased to Osiris, the Judge.
6. The deceased, who is in the act of being judged.
7. THOTH, presiding over and making a record of the weights.
8. ANUBIS, presiding over and managing the balance in the scale of Justice.
9. CERBERUS, watching the gates of Hades.
10. HORUS conducting the deceased to have his actions weighed in the balance.
11. The Deceased.
12. Wife or sister of deceased, who accompanies him to where the scale of justice is.

Horus conducts the deceased, who sometimes is accompanied by his sister or wife, to the region of Armenti. Cerberus is present as guardian of the gates near the place where the scale of Justice is erected.

Anubis, the director of the weight; having placed a vase representing the good actions of the deceased in one

---

* Diodorus Sicul. Hist., lib. i., cap. 92.

scale and the emblem of truth in the other.  This reminds us of the interpretation by Daniel of the handwriting on the Babylonian palace, Thou art weighed in the balance and found wanting—proceeds to ascertain the claims for admission.

Thoth inscribes an account of them on his tablet, which Horus, son of Osiris, presents to his father and judge.

Four Genii of Armenti stand on a lotus flower.  Behind the judge stands Harpocrates, type of youth and new life, showing that he must be born again to enter into eternal bliss.  Sometimes Osiris is attended by Isis and Nepttys.

Above sit the forty-two assessors, in two lines, the complete number mentioned by Diodorus, who had assisted in judging the dead.  They are supposed to represent the forty-two crimes from which a virtuous man was expected to be free when judged in a future state.  These are distinct from the thirty-six demons, mentioned by Origen : these presided over the human body, which was divided into the same number of parts, each appointed to one of them, and they were often invoked to have the infirmities of the peculiar member immediately under their protection.  But they may perhaps have some reference or call to mind the four-and-twenty elders mentioned in the fourth chapter and fourth verse and nineteenth chapter and fourth verse of Revelation, as the four Genii of Armenti appear to have some analogy to the four beasts who were present with them before the judgment-seat.

Harpocrates and Horus were both sons of Isis.  But Harpocrates was born to Osiris by Isis after his death, and therefore is distinct from Horus.  Harpocrates is sometimes seen with his finger in his mouth, denoting youth, mostly in a sitting posture, but sometimes he stands erect, as in the figure.

Osiris, the judge of the dead, pronounces the sentence after Horus presents the findings of Thoth, admitting the virtuous in his presence, in the mansion of the blessed. There before the entrance sits Harpocrates, the type of youth and new life; also a hideous monster, the proto- type of Cerberus, sometimes called the " devourer of the wicked." He guards the gates of Hades. The killing of the great serpent, the emblem of sin, the binding of the wicked, and their punishment in fire. These paintings were made in the tombs of Egypt over two thousand years before the birth of the Saviour. These almighty truths in the beginning were known only to God, who always appeared to be greatly interested in Egypt. It was there he first made himself known to the Israelites, and at the first did visit the Gentiles to take out of them a people for his name. Abraham, on his visit into Egypt, was so fascinated with the modesty and beauty of the women, that he took one for a wife.

And it was not only in Egypt that Judgment and Immortality was taught. To Pedro Jose de Arriaga, a Jesuit, who spent over a year, from February 1617 to July 1618, among the idolatrous Peruvians, we are in- debted for the most reliable history of that ancient peo- ple. He says, " Faith in the immortality of the soul was the fundamental idea among all Peruvian nations. They also believed their god *Pachacamac*, and in some prov- inces *Con*, acted as judge of mankind." (Peruvian An- tiquities, page 151.)

It was to Egypt he directed Joseph and Mary to flee

for safety with the young child Jesus when Herod was planning his death. Yes, the fame of Egypt was known and honored throughout the earth.* Men hailing from that country were looked upon as the most favored of mankind. Moses was not the only one who profited by the wisdom of Egypt; the early Grecian philosophers returning from that country were doubly reverenced, but the Jews were so blinded through greed for the things of this life that they failed to comprehend a future, so frequently foreshadowed by their prophets.

Independent of the Jews, all the pagan world had a common tradition of the Creation, the Flood, and the promise that the seed of the woman should bruise the serpent's head, or that death itself should die. We might give quotations from Greek and Roman poets showing that long before Christ was born, the pagan world was in expectation of the advent of some great personage. Yes, this blessed doctrine of the Resurrection crossed the Jewish dispensation, arriving at the border scarred with Egyptian idolatry, yet the Saviour did not reject it. No prophets then lived to endorse it, as the day of Jewish inspiration had closed with the Book of Malachi, written four hundred years before. But around the dying embers of the materialistic Jewish rites, Jesus proclaimed the heavenly doctrine. And on Calvary, amidst darkness and earthquakes, stamped it with immortality and sealed it with his blood.

RESURRECTION FLOWER—found in the tombs of Egyptian kings, typical of their resurrection from the dead.

We give on next page a letter from Mr. George W.

---

* Euclid, Plato, and Homer, made it their home.

Huffnagle to the author. Mr. Huffnagle's brother spent about thirty years in India, as Consul-General of the United States. Being a man of learning, and withal an antiquarian, he collected and sent home many rare and valuable curiosities; among them was this Rose, which he procured in Egypt while on an exploring expedition among the Egyptian tombs. Something similar has been found in California. A writer in a California paper remarks: " On the rocks of high mountains, where rain seldom falls, grows the rose 'Everlasting.' It blooms only once a year, has leaves at no other time; it can be placed in a box and kept for years, when, if placed in a bowl of water for twenty-four hours, it will bloom. Put back in the box, it will remain unchanged during other years."

" Deacon Dye—Dear Sir : A lady placed on exhibition at the Pennsylvania Horticultural Society at Philadelphia, an *Anastatica* or *Hirrochantis*, or *Resurrection flower*. This plant is from Palestine, and is called by the natives *Kaf Maryam* or *Mary's Hand.*

" Bayard Taylor, in his travels through that land, terms it the *Rose of Jericho.* In its usual state. it is a dry, withered looking bunch of twigs, about the size of an average walnut, but when placed in water, it expands to about five inches in diameter.

" Very few specimens of this are known.

" Baron Humboldt, and Professor Wood, the celebrated botanist of New York, each possessed one. They were taken from the *Egyptian Mummies*, and though shut out from all life for *three thousand years*, they bloomed when placed in water.

" There is a peculiar propriety in the same land that witnessed the Resurrection of our *Lord* and *Saviour*, giving us the flower that seems to be immortal.

" Yours respectfully,

" Geo. W. Huffnagle.

Springdale, New Hope, Bucks Co., Pa., Sept. 25, 1868."

Important letter from Prof. CHARLES BRYANT, who was sent to Alaska by the United States government to examine into the condition of the Indians in that territory. He also furnished the author two valuable portraits, to be found in the body of the book.

FAIRHAVEN, December 11th, 1869.

'To J. S. DYE, Esq.—Sir : I have the pleasure of sending you the following account of the natives inhabiting the northwest shores of New Holland.

''While lying at anchor among the Rosemary Islands, a cluster of low sand-banks off the coast of New Holland, for the purpose of taking humpback whales, a group of these miserable beings were wandering about these low sandy islands. There were three of them—one a male, about five feet three or four inches, and two females, about four feet six inches in height. They were so besmeared all over with what looked like yellow ochre, that it was difficult to clearly define their natural color, which appeared a sooty black. Their bodies had an emaciated appearance, their limbs being imperfectly developed, and little larger at the junction of the body than the ankles and wrists. They were very pot-bellied ; they had a scant growth of coarse curly hair on the head ; the male a few straggling hairs on the chin, and had the hair on his head tied in a knot with a pointed stick three-eighths of an inch in diameter and six or seven inches long. They wore no clothing, seemed to have no language, uttering short, shrill sounds, not unlike the yelping of a dog. . One of the ship's crew spent some time trying to teach one of them to utter articulate sounds in vain. They had a dry log of the Pendenis tree, five or six feet long, and six · or eight inches in diameter, slightly narrowed in the middle, astride of which they sat in the water and paddled themselves with their hands from one island to another, the tide often carrying them some distance from land. When met by the boats, they would invariably beg for water by yelping out, throwing their heads back, making signs of dropping sea-water in their open mouths. They would drink large quantities, and we soon learned to give no more than for one at a time, for if a full bucket were given for all three, the first one that got it swallowed all the contents. When we first arrived at the islands, they were subsisting on green turtle, which they caught by wading on the shallow reefs, and killing them with the stick the male carried in his hair, by thrusting it through the eyes into the brain. When dead, the body was broken with stones, and the flesh devoured raw. After whales had been taken and their carcasses drifted on shore, they remained near them when hungry, tore off the putrid lean flesh with their teeth like dogs, eating until gorged ; then rolling themselves in the sand, dozed and slept nearly all the time. One thing puzzled me much : the sharks were so plenty that, in fishing, it was hardly possible to get a whole one out of the water for them, yet these natives paddled among them without injury.

''SITKA.—The Indians occupying the eastern portion of the territory of Alaska, appear to be descendants of the former occupants of a more southern latitude, having reached their present location by migrating up the shore until checked by the coast range of mountains from further progress ; here they occupy the coast slope and islands, living in tribes for the better obtaining of food ; but all claiming a common origin under the name of Kolosh. These Sitkas are living on Baranoff Island, where the Russian Fur Company had their principal depot called Sitka, from these Indians. They are below the average height of the European race, of a dark sooty color, have full faces, broad backs, and stout shoulders, but somewhat light limbs; live in large wooden houses built of timber and boards, exhibiting considerable degree of skill in finishing them. Unlike most Indians, the men do all the outdoor labor, while their women lounge round the streets of the town. They also manifest much skill in working silver, melting coin, and manufacturing it into jewelry and ornaments for their women—such as ear-rings and bracelets : the latter they chase in a manner to compare favorably with more skilful engravers at home. They also carve wood, ivory, and stone, in various patterns, and wear them as charms. From the best data obtainable, they inherit the knowledge from their ancestors, possessing it at the time of the Peruvian occupation. Their religion, like most savages, is a dark superstition, and manifests itself more in efforts to propitiate the agents of evil, than do right and defy them. Both sexes paint their faces—red and black being the favorite colors ; the young belles frequently appearing in the streets of the town with faces polished and shining like a boot, while the beaux appear with red rings around the eyes and mouth.

"They burn their dead by enclosing them in a pyre of wooden logs ; the female relatives sit by and wail, while the old men stand and drum on the ground with long staves, chanting a droning, monotonous song, beating time to it. After burning, the ashes are gathered and enclosed in a box and placed on stakes, two feet above ground, near the dwelling. The box is sometimes ornamented with rude sketches of the human face.

"The enclosed photograph is of an Aleutian child, about eight years old, born on the island of Onalaska ; her parents being poor, she was given by them to a merchant trading there, who adopted her and sent her to his mother in Russia : on her way through New York, this photograph was taken and sent to me by her patron—she having been a pet of mine during my sojourn on St. Paul's Island, in Behring Sea. She is a very fair representative of an Aleutian child.

"The long chain of islands extending from the end of the Alaskan peninsular westward nearly to Kamschatka, a distance of nine hundred miles, are inhabited by a branch or family of Asiatic origin, calling themselves Al-e-utes. They differ too widely from their neighbors on the main land to the west of them, to belong to that branch of the Mongolian family. They are undoubtedly the descendants of Japanese mariners, whose vessels have been wrecked and borne by the ocean current to these islands, probably at different times : one such vessel has arrived there three years since, and the living sailors, composing her crew, were returned by the Russians. They are of smaller stature than the European, and vary from nearly white to olive complexion ; very fair ; have the arched brow and almond-shaped eye of the Asiatic, but not the high cheekbones of the pure Mongolian ; are light limbed and active in their movements ; are all Christianized, being members of the Greek church ; live in villages in well-organized communities ; supporting their churches and schools, can generally read and write the Russian language, and understand the simple rules of arithmetic. There being no wood on these islands, the natives build their houses of turf, and thatch with the long grass growing on the island.

"They dress in European style, and are a very mild, peaceful people, closely following the teachings of their church creed and the commandments. Quarrels and theft are unheard of among them, and it is impossible for a stranger to go among them without becoming deeply interested in them and their future welfare. They subsist by fishing and hunting the Sea Otter.

"Yours to command,

"CHARLES BRYANT."

www.ingramcontent.com/pod-product-compliance
Lightning Source LLC
Chambersburg PA
CBHW032110010726
47493CB00008B/2532